GLIMMER

ALSO BY PATRICIA BOW

GLIMMER

PATRICIA BOW

Published by Patricia Bow
www.execulink.com/~thebows/patricia.htm

Distributed by Lulu Press
www.lulu.com

This book was first published in 2010 by Cora Verlag GmbH under the title *See der Schwarzen Sterne,* in German translation. *Glimmer* is the author's original (but revised and expanded) English text.

Goblin Postman icon created by Patricia Bow

Cover image: "Ethereal Glow" by Sara Carter, adapted and used in accordance with her Creative Commons license. (https://www.flickr.com/photos/australianshepherds/5455318247/)

This book, which is all about blood

— bad, good, and shared —

is for my sisters and brothers:

Deanna

Gordon

Margaret

Dorothy

Bette

Edward

Prologue

NO ONE NOW LIVING can tell you what it was like to dance in the Glimmer Lake pavilion. You will only hear what the survivors told their children: how on a warm summer evening it was a magical place, lilting with music and laughter. From far across the lake it shone on the water like a golden lantern. Its faint distant music wove enchantment.

But that was long ago.

Now it stands silent and deserted. Ice drapes its broken arches. Its only light is the moon.

In the precise centre of this derelict space, something gleams in mid-air. The golden object is shaped like a sun with rays, and is no bigger than a thumbnail. A tiny diamond winks at its heart.

It might be an earring pendant or a charm torn from a bracelet. Lost, perhaps, nearly a century ago. Its polished surface reflects all sides of the ruined room as it slowly revolves, first one way and then the other, as if hung by a thread from the ceiling.

Only, there is no thread. And no ceiling.

Ice-crusted timbers show on the golden surface and slide away. A face comes into view. The lips do not move.

Where is she?

Instantly the face is gone, replaced by another image. The view is of a street at twilight. Streetlights gleam on icy sidewalks and yards mounded with snow. The pendant's golden face lends the scene an amber tint. The straight lines of a house, its door and windows, swirl around the inset diamond.

Still nothing.

A smudge moves at the edge of the reflected scene.

There! At last!

The smudge grows larger. It becomes a human figure muffled in thick coat, scarf and toque, trudging along the street while hefting two heavy bags. The figure, now plainly a young woman, stops on the sidewalk and stands still for a moment, looking up at the house, before picking a careful way up the icy walk. She climbs the porch stairs and again pauses before pressing the bell, grasping the knob, and thumping the panels of the door.

Look around! Look at me!

There: the girl feels something. She looks over her shoulder and then up and down the street.

Here! I am here!

Nothing, no contact, not yet. Not ready.

The image of the street disappears. The sunburst pendant revolves slowly, throwing out spangles of golden light. Once, twice, three times it turns, and it's gone.

Chapter 1

STELLA CAME HOME to Glimmer in a clear blue December twilight. Away from the main drag the streets were quiet and almost deserted.

But not without life or colour. Even on Bluejay Road, out on the edge of town, there were signs of celebration. Six of the seven houses along the frozen south shore of Glimmer Lake were outlined in Christmas lights. More lights glittered in the pines and cedars that hedged each house against the wind. Lit windows glowed from behind drawn curtains.

The only dark house on the street was Molly's, second from the inner end. No Christmas lights here. But Stella wasn't surprised to see a big wreath of holly on the front door. Holly was totally pagan, as Molly had explained in her last text message.

Stella stood for a freezing minute on the sidewalk, looking up at the windows that were like eyes closed in sleep. From here the house appeared unchanged, except for — an emphatic change, this — a painted green-and-white sign in the living room window, to the right of the front door. MAGIC BY THE LAKE it said, in large Celtic-style letters. Below that hung a card that said SORRY, WE'RE CLOSED.

She gave herself a shake, slithered up the icy walk to the steps, and climbed the steps to the small, square porch. The light on the ceiling was a box of heavy cut glass, the same as she remembered. It was unlit. The door was also unchanged: varnished oak panels topped by a semi-circle of leaded glass. She rose up on tiptoes and peered in.

Nothing to see.

She hesitated. Sniffed contempt at herself. Stabbed a mittened hand at the doorbell. Waited. No answer, no sound of feet inside. She grasped the knob. Locked. She thumped on the door. No good.

"All right, Molly, where've you got to? Not at the bus stop and not here. Come *on*, you knew I was coming!"

And where were all the other people? Inside at their dinner tables? She looked over her shoulder. The street still looked empty, yet somebody was out there watching her. She turned around and scanned up and down. Someone was looking at her, she'd swear to it. The sense of eyes on her face was as definite as a hand's touch. But the Nosy Parker was invisible, or hiding. Behind one of those curtained windows across the road, probably.

Lowering her backpack and flight bag to the porch floor, she rummaged in a zippered pocket, found the key Molly had sent ("In case I'm out when you arrive.") and unlocked the door. Chimes tinkled as the door swung open and closed behind her. Without looking, she reached for the light switch to the right of the door and flipped it.

The light switch was where it had always been, but everything else was changed. ("I've done some renovating," Molly had said.) Inside the door was a small, white rectangular lobby, empty except for a wicker umbrella stand in the near right corner. No surprises there.

But the lobby, as Stella remembered it, was walled on the right and open to the hallway in front, with a coat closet on the left. Now there was a wide archway on her right and a wall in front. The closet had become an open alcove with hooks for coats and three rubber boot trays below.

Stella dropped her bags on the floor, pulled off her boots and set them on a tray, then padded in her hand-knitted Fair Isle socks (a present from Molly) through the new archway into what used to be the living room.

Here again, completely different. Though not unexpected. Stella gazed around at the shelves of folded scarves, racks of hanging crystals and rows of DVDs. Silver and amber jewellery shone on black velvet in a glass-fronted cabinet next to the cash terminal. There was a lounge area on the east side of the room, with a cotton-upholstered sofa facing the fireplace across an oval braided rug, an easy chair and a recliner at either side, and low shelves of books close at hand. A sign propped up on one of the shelf units said BOOK NOOK – ALL BOOKS FOR SALE.

The room smelled of beeswax and sandalwood and something else, something more pungent and less pleasant.

Stella gazed around, lips pursed, silently whistling. To think of Molly — Molly! — running an actual business! It looked as if it was thriving, too. Perhaps because it was the only Wiccan gift shop in Glimmer. Possibly the only one in a large chunk of northeastern Ontario.

"Molly? I'm here!" The house had a hollow, deserted sound. "Molly!" No answer. No Molly.

Stella went back into the lobby, struggled out of her parka and scarf and hung them on hooks, pulled off her toque and raked fingers through her short brown hair. A small gold pendant shaped like a five-pointed star slipped free of her sweater and swung on a thin gold chain. She tucked it back in. Then left her bags where they'd dropped and went exploring.

In the wall of the shop next to the archway was a panelled wooden door with a brass sign screwed into the wood at eye level. The sign said PRIVATE. The door looked both strange and familiar. Stella remembered after a moment that it belonged here, but it had always stood open, modestly back against the wall, hardly noticed. Now it was staring her in the face, as if guarding something.

Locked? She opened it. Not locked. And yes, here was the front hall leading to the kitchen, and the stairs to the second floor. Made private, separate from the shop. So there was method in Molly's renovating madness.

She closed the door again and walked across the shop. A pair of leaded glass doors behind the cash desk, on the north side, led into what used to be the dining room. The old mahogany table was still there, too big and heavy to be moved out except in pieces. The same table where they used to eat dinner together, the five of them: Mom, Dad, Travis, Molly, and Stella, under the brass filigree lamp that was also still there.

Now the table was covered with plastic bins full of vertical file folders. The folders had labels like "Invoices, Paid" and "Orders, Outstanding" and "Suppliers, Handcrafts." A computer squatted among the bins with a swivel chair in front of it. Grey file cabinets and steel shelving full of cardboard boxes stood along the walls. The north wall looked wrong, out of place, until Stella saw that part of the room had been dry-walled off to make washrooms. Two white doors were set in the new wall side by side, one painted with the silhouette of an armoured knight, the other with the silhouette of a coiled dragon. That would be Molly's idea of a joke.

Stella was glad she could see the humour. She'd been looking forward to this visit, yet at the same time she'd been dreading it, seeing the old house again for the first time after half her lifetime away. Dreading a rush of sadness.

But looking down at the old table and up at the brass lamp, she knew that whatever had been home to her in this house was gone. Maybe it went away all those years ago, that snowy night when Mom and Dad's car slid off Shore Road into a tree. The snowmobiler who had likely caused the accident, the police said, judging by the tracks, had never been found. Was probably still living in Glimmer, fat and happy and guilt-free.

Stella shook away the thought and pushed through a door on the left into the kitchen. This room didn't look anything like the way she remembered it. The scarred pine table was gone, replaced by glass-topped wicker. Molly had painted the wood-veneer cabinets sunshine yellow. She'd painted the white walls sky-blue, and splashed them with childlike shapes of flowers and birds and stars. Ladybug-shaped magnets on the refrigerator held internet printouts of recipes for Indian chai and pumpkin bread.

Here the smell mixture included cloves and curry powder. Stella hadn't been feeling hungry — too tired — but now remembered that the last thing she'd put in her stomach was an overcooked, dried-out cheeseburger eaten in Toronto's Bay Street bus terminal six hours ago.

She opened the refrigerator. Not much choice, unless you really liked alfalfa sprouts and tofu. Something smelled off, too. She opened a carton of milk and wrinkled her nose. This should have been finished up two days ago.

She poured the milk down the sink drain, rinsed the carton, flattened it and dropped it into the recycling bin. Maybe that was why Molly was out: buying fresh milk. "And real food, too, I hope!" You'd think she'd leave a light on, though.

Might as well see where I'll be sleeping. The door that opened from the kitchen to the front hall and led to the stairs was still there, for a wonder.

Stella flicked on the light in the stairwell and climbed, stroking her hand along the polished oak banister. More changes up here. The upstairs hall used to be off-white, with small framed watercolour landscapes between the doors. Molly had changed the off-white to dusky plum and hung a magnificent medallion quilt on the stairwell wall.

The upper hallway led at one end to a door with a tall oval window that opened onto a tiny balcony on the north side of the house, overlooking the back yard and the lake. A bathroom and three bedrooms were strung along the hall. As kids, Molly and Stella had shared the back bedroom, next to the balcony. Travis used to have the one at the front corner over the porch. Mom and Dad had the big one that took up most of the east side.

Travis still couldn't understand what had possessed Molly, once her small legacy from their parents had come through, to go back and buy the old house after all these years away. "Homesick," Molly said.

Stella got it. Molly had always loved her memories of Glimmer: the little school with its grassy yard, the teachers, the childhood friendships. Summers swimming and exploring the woods, winters skating and building snow forts, fall days with bright leaves flying along the sunlit streets, the encircling hills purple with wild asters, nights scented with wood smoke.

For a moment memory filled the house like distant laughter. Then it faded, leaving emptiness. And a sense of something or someone listening.

Stella stood still in the upstairs hall. She knew suddenly that something was wrong. Her hand flew up to touch her star pendant through the wool of her sweater. *Think!* It wasn't the new colours or smells or the moved walls, or the different things hanging on the walls. What was it?

Walking quietly along the hall, she opened the door of the back bedroom. The strange, pungent smell was stronger here. Herbs? Turpentine? The room was dark, with only a faint blue glow leaking in through the white-curtained window.

Her hand went to the light switch to the left of the door, but never flipped it. A shadow surged from behind the door and slid past her. In passing it hit her shoulder. She spun and staggered. Suddenly there were arms around her, pulling her upright. She drew breath to scream and a hand clamped over her mouth.

Pitching wildly from side to side, Stella dragged her attacker with her and they fell against the wall. The switch clicked. Light burst out. She stared up into the face a few inches above her own.

Chapter 2

EYES, BRIGHT BROWN in the sudden glare, widened at her from under a mop of coffee-brown hair. "Please don't scream!" he gasped. "I'm not a mugger, I swear it!"

Stella screamed as loud as she could — which, with her mouth muffled, wasn't much louder than an angry "Mmff!" She lunged again. He tightened his hold.

"Please! I won't hurt you! I— ow!" He yanked his hand away. "You bit me!"

"Just for starters!" Her knee slammed into his thigh. He yelled and let go and she leaped for the doorway.

"Wait! Don't call the police! Please!"

Something in his voice reached her. If she hadn't been so scared and furious she would have called it honesty. And desperation. She paused at the top of the stairs, ready to plunge downward if he so much as moved a finger.

He stayed where he was, in the doorway to the back bedroom, three strides away. He looked about her own age, eighteen. She'd never met him before, that was for sure, yet he looked teasingly familiar. She pointed a trembling forefinger at him. "Give me one good reason not to call the cops!"

"Because I, well, I'm not a criminal. Really."

"You broke in —"

"That's just it, I didn't!"

"Oh no? Then how'd you get in?"

"I have a key. See?" He fished it out of his coat pocket and dangled it by its ring from his forefinger.

"Where'd you get that?"

"My brother had it. Molly gave it to him."

It clicked. "Now I know why you look familiar."

Molly had texted a message four days earlier, with a photo attached. "Here's me and the boyfriend, Edge West," she wrote. "Edge is short for Edward George. Gorgeous, no? He has his problems, but who doesn't? And who better than me to straighten him out?"

The man in the photo was maybe twenty, a year older than Molly. He was handsome in a pale-faced, dark-eyed, broody way. *Problems? Oh, Molly. Not another hurt puppy!*

"You look like Edge West, sort of," Stella said now. "I've seen his picture. You must be his kid brother."

"Right, and you're Molly's kid sister. You look like her. Sort of." His mouth relaxed, his eyes warmed. "Stella, right? I'm Mike."

She gave him a look that said *I'm not pleased to meet you.* Then she stepped back across the hall and stood facing him. "You had no right to use that key." She held out a hand, palm up.

"I know." He dropped it into her hand. "I, um, better go now." He started forward.

"Hold on!" She planted her feet and blocked his way to the stairs. "You haven't said what you're doing in Molly's house."

"I... uh... I was trying to find out what happened to Edge. If they went away together."

"Wait a minute. Molly's away? Away where?"

"I don't know. Don't you?"

"She invited me for the Christmas break. She's supposed to be here."

"I haven't seen Edge for two days. Or Molly either. Neither has anybody else. I've asked."

"Two days!" Her stomach went cold. She frowned at him. "So why were you here?"

"Looking for a clue, I guess." He stuck his hands in his jeans pockets. "Like, if she left some note. Or if he did. I didn't find anything."

That could have been true. Still, she didn't feel inclined to cut him any slack. She stepped aside and tilted her head at the stairs.

"Right. I'm on my way."

She stayed close behind him down the stairs, through the private door at the bottom, into the shop and around the corner into the lobby and out the front door. (He'd been wearing his boots the whole time, but must have wiped them carefully before starting upstairs.) On the step outside he turned and opened his mouth. She slammed the door. Well-meaning or no, he didn't deserve any better.

Stella put the extra key away in a drawer under the cash terminal. She checked the locks on the front and back doors, and hoped Molly hadn't given out any more keys.

By now it was six o'clock. She dug her phone out of her backpack, checked the time, subtracted the three hours' difference between Ontario and British Columbia, and tapped in the numbers for a call to Nanaimo. For Travis it was still mid-afternoon. He was at work.

"Macmillan Consulting. Travis Macmillan speaking," said the brisk voice on the other end.

"Trav! Guess what!"

"Stella? Why are you calling now?"

"Hey, dear brother, I just arrived in Glimmer safe and sound! Don't you care? Never mind, there's something funny going on here. Have you heard from Molly since I left?"

"Of course not. Why would Molly contact me?"

Stella flicked her eyes up, exasperated. "Not you. I thought she might've left a message for me. She's not here. She hasn't been around for two days."

A silence, then a heavy sigh. "Isn't that just like Molly! Where's she gone?"

"I don't *know* where she's gone or I wouldn't be asking! And no, it isn't just like her."

Their lives together had not always been peaceful in the ten years since their parents' death. There had been stormy episodes. Travis had been only eighteen when he became, as he put it, the head of the family. He had taken his responsibilities very seriously. Molly had pushed back, hard and often. Travis had never really understood or forgiven her.

"I mean, it wouldn't be like her to ask me here, and then just go off and leave me in the lurch. She'd tell me what was up."

"But she didn't, did she? Come on home, Stella."

"Come home? Travis, do you realize how long I've been travelling? Sixteen hours!"

"Including the four hours shopping in downtown Toronto?"

She ignored that. "A turboprop, a plane, a bus. And then I had to walk to Molly's house from the bus stop, lugging my gear. I'm totally wiped! No way I'm going to turn around and come straight home. Besides, there's not another bus out of here until tomorrow morning."

"Come home tomorrow, then. Look, I can't talk now. I'm expecting a client." The line went dead. Stella stuck her tongue out at the phone, thumbed it off and hooked it on the waistband of her jeans.

What now? The silence and emptiness of the house closed around her. The sense of *something wrong* intensified. She thought of the milk that had gone sour. It might mean nothing. Still...

It was worth a search. At best she would find nothing. She poked around under the counter beside the cash terminal, and in the shelves behind. There was another phone here, a land line. Then she looked around the dining room / office, under the table, in the filing cabinets. You never knew where Molly might put things.

Last stop: upstairs, the back bedroom. And there it was, hanging on a hook in the closet: a large shoulder bag pieced from multicoloured hand-woven fabrics. Among the jumble of things inside were Molly's health card, social insurance, credit cards, driver's licence, all her ID. And a wallet with money.

But no phone. That was encouraging. Wherever Molly was, she had her phone with her. Stella pulled out her own phone and speed-dialled Molly's number, mentally preparing a list of reproaches. Molly's light, warm voice answered. "Hi! I'm Molly Macmillan, and I'm not here right now. Talk to me!" *Click.*

"Molly! Where the heck are you? It's me, Stella. I'm here at the house. For heaven's sake call!"

Stella paced the bedroom for a few minutes, chewing her lip and trying to make sense of the situation. Then ran downstairs again and pulled on her coat, boots, toque, scarf, and mitts and stepped out onto the porch. She locked the door carefully and picked her way back down the icy path to the street. The wind hissed in the pines and scoured her cheeks. She'd forgotten how cold it got in these parts.

Food first, she thought. *Real food, not alfalfa sprouts. And good hot coffee. I'm so famished I can't think straight, that's my trouble.*

Bluejay Road was still deserted. Now it had that unreal look of a winter street at night. The harsh artificial light flattened everything like a stage set, casting black shadows and hiding the stars. Stella turned left and walked along the roadway toward what Glimmerites called their downtown.

And there it was again: the feeling of being watched. Different now, though. There was an edge to it: a sting of malice that was new. Stella gave herself a shake and told herself to *shape up!* Getting spooked by every little thing was not going to help at all.

To prove to herself there was nobody staring balefully at her back, she whirled around and searched the street with her eyes.

That didn't help. The wind was stirring the bushes, tossing shadows. There, between those two houses: you'd think that clump of darkness was some animal slinking after her under the cedars. She could even imagine the narrowing of gleaming eyes.

She laughed aloud and mentally slapped herself; pulled her toque down over her ears and her scarf up over her chin and walked on. By the time she reached Queen Street her hands had almost stopped shaking.

Chapter 3

QUEEN STREET was all lit up. Pine-and-ribbon arches studded with gold, red and green lights spanned the roadway. Every store window was bright with colourful Christmas decorations. Carol tunes danced out of every opening door.

A new doughnut shop, all neon and chrome, stood at the corner of Market Street and Queen. Stella walked past it and pushed open the steamy glass door of Bonnie's Good Eats. This old place hadn't changed a bit. She stopped inside the closed door and breathed in, while opening her jacket. It took her back ten years in a heartbeat, that smell of fresh coffee and fried onions and damp overcoats.

The room fell silent as she threaded her way between tables to the bar and perched on an empty stool. Then the talk started up again, but more quietly. Lots of ears bent this way. Well, why not? She was new — she was news.

"Hi! What'll ya have?" That sounded like Bonnie Orr, but the woman who faced her across the counter, wearing a red cotton shirt with "Bonnie" embroidered in white on the pocket, looked nothing like the Bonnie that Stella was expecting.

She remembered, as a little girl, being frightened of Mrs. Orr's high-piled, stiff, coal-black hair, her large white teeth, her loud laugh, and her ferocious horn-rimmed glasses. And that scary way she had of turning a grim, grey eye on a child who hadn't cleaned her plate. In whispers to Molly, Stella used to call her "Mrs. Ogre."

"Where's Bonnie?" Stella asked now.

"You're looking at her!" At Stella's raised eyebrows, the woman grinned. "I'm her granddaughter. We happen to have the same name."

This Bonnie was young, sunny-faced, and crowned with very short sunset-pink hair. "My gran retired a few years ago. She still owns the place. I run it." She pointed an egg-flipper. "Wait! Don't tell me. You're Stella, aren't you? Molly's sister."

"That's right. I—"

"I knew it! You look kinda like her. Only thinner, and your hair's straight instead of curly. Molly turned up yet?"

"No. I'm trying to find out..." Conversations silenced all around. She leaned forward and lowered her voice. "Um, if anyone knows where she is."

"Molly goes her own road. You here to eat or just talk?"

"Eat!" She sat up straight. "I'll have a bowl of chilli, grilled cheese and bacon sandwich, dill pickle on the side, fries, and a cup of coffee, double cream, no sugar."

Bonnie slapped the counter. "That's cool!" She grinned at Stella. "Your sister says my meals are poison — all that cholesterol. She likes my bean soup, though." She waved the egg-flipper. "I'll bring it. You take that empty booth by the window."

Sitting in the high-backed booth, shielded from the view of half the room, Stella felt less like a bug under a microscope. She wondered if that was what Bonnie'd had in mind.

A large postcard stuck in the cruet between the ketchup and the vinegar caught her eye. FESTIVAL OF LIGHTS, it said. CELEBRATE THE SEASON AT THE NEW PAVILION — DANCE THE NIGHT AWAY. Then a date, December 21, four days from now. Below that, a pen-and-ink drawing of a building on the lakeshore: a fantasy of leaping arches, slim columns, and big windows under a roof that was all curves and wooden filigree.

It took a minute for Stella to remember where she'd seen an image like this before. When Bonnie set down a heaped plate in front of her, Stella held up the card. "Isn't that..."

"Right! They rebuilt that old ruin and we're having a party to celebrate. And Bonnie's Good Eats is in charge of the catering. Isn't that awesome?" Bonnie filled Stella's mug from a steaming carafe. "Gran thinks they shouldn't have done it, rebuilt the pavilion, I mean. Disrespectful of the dead, she says. Molly says the same thing. She says they're asking for trouble, but everybody else—"

"Listen, about Molly.... "

Bonnie slid into the opposite seat and lowered her voice. "Hey, I can tell you're worried. But, you know what I think? You've heard of Edge West?"

"The boyfriend?"

"Right. Well, he's gone too. So, naturally, people are putting two and two together." She sat back and winked. "One and one, I mean. Maybe they'll come back married!" She put a hand on Stella's wrist. "And speak of the devil, or the devil's brother, look out there!"

Stella looked out the window and jumped. Mike West was looking at her from about twelve inches away. She wondered how long he had been out there on the sidewalk, glowering at her through the glass while she studied the Festival of Lights card. And why?

"Have you two guys met?" Bonnie glanced from the window to Stella's face. "He's looking at you like he knows you. Don't worry, Mike's okay, he's not like Edge. I mean, everybody knows Edge is wild. He'd do anything. Once he climbed the water tower in the dead of night and painted a huge skull and crossbones on the side in green paint, for a joke. The picture was in the Toronto newspapers. But Mike's not like that. He's got a good head on his shoulders."

Bonnie slid out of the booth, gave Stella a cheerful pat on the shoulder, and whisked away. When Stella looked out the window again, Mike was walking toward the door of the restaurant. Half a minute later he was inside and standing beside her booth.

"Okay if I sit?"

Stella picked up her fork and started in on the chilli. "Why?"

"I need to apologize. And I need to explain."

"Have you been following me?"

"Me? No!"

"Because I'm getting the feeling that somebody's following me. And I don't like it."

"It wasn't me! I just happened to see you in here." He frowned at the window. "I wonder... but..."

Nothing more was coming out of him. She studied his face, which looked no less desperately worried than it had earlier. She pointed at the seat opposite. "Sit."

He sat. "About grabbing you, at the house, that was out of line, I'm sorry," he said rapidly. "And it sure wasn't smart, but I wasn't thinking straight, okay? I'd knocked you over and I didn't want you to hurt yourself, so I grabbed you, and then I was scared you'd go off the deep end and scream and call the police, so I..."

"Panicked." Stella took a bite of pickle.

"Yeah. I lost it. I'm sorry."

"Okay." Stella put down the pickle and gave him a straight look. "But if you *ever* grab me like that again—"

"Never!" He held up both hands, palms out. "I swear!"

"Well..." There seemed no reason not to believe him. Besides, she was starting to feel sorry for him. He had a lean and frayed-at-the-edges look, as if he had been sleeping badly and missing meals. She pushed half of the sandwich toward him. "Hungry?"

He shook his head, but picked up her coffee mug and absently nursed the hot crockery in his hands, as if they were cold. "It's the police: they're the problem."

"The police! Why?"

"See, Edge has a rep." He leaned forward earnestly. "He's always been a bit of a bad boy, at least since... well, a few years. The local OPP hate him, they think he's trouble."

"And is he?"

Mike gestured with the mug. "Sometimes. Not as much as they make out."

"Oh, Molly," Stella murmured.

"When I went to the detachment office today to report Edge missing, they just smirked. Wild West, gone again. But I *know* Edge wouldn't go off like that, for two whole days, without telling me."

"That's exactly what I've been saying about Molly!"

"Really? I always thought she was... um." He flushed.

"Wild?" Stella looked at him dangerously. "Like Edge?"

"Well, no. Um... more, well, carefree. A free spirit."

"An airhead, you mean."

"Uh, well, yeah." By now he was apple-red.

"Well, she is, sometimes. But not nearly as much as she likes to pretend." Stella took back her mug. "And I know she wouldn't go off like that without a word to me. Besides, I found something. Something that's got me worried." She told him about Molly's bag with all her ID, still in the closet. "She'd never leave that behind!"

"Yes!" Mike thumped the table with his fist. "That's new evidence! Now they'll have to take this seriously!"

Stella pushed aside her half-eaten supper and pulled out her wallet. "Let's go!"

Chapter 4

"WELL, THAT WASN'T a complete waste of time. But close." Stella let the door of the Ontario Provincial Police detachment office slam behind her.

Sergeant Reg Yantzi, OPP Glimmer, had been polite and patient. But he'd refused to start a search, and he clearly grudged wasting valuable time on a case that was not a case.

"But she doesn't answer her phone," Stella persisted. "And what about the bag she left behind? All her ID and money and credit cards. That proves she wasn't planning to go anywhere!"

"People don't always plan," Yantzi said, in a tone that meant, *People like Molly.*

"Molly's not stupid! Aren't you going to do anything?"

"I've scanned that photo you showed me and I'll circulate it to the other detachment offices in the region. That's the most I can do."

Stella guessed it was better than nothing.

Outside in the street, she gave the closed door a scowl before turning away. Mike stuck his hands in his parka pockets. "You did fine. Better than me. They didn't offer to circulate Edge's photo."

"What am I supposed to do now?" she growled.

"Get some sleep. Nothing more you can do today." He added, "I'll walk you home."

"Thanks, but I'll be fine. This is Glimmer, not Toronto!"

"No trouble. It's on my way."

Stella thought of the shadowy shape she'd imagined slinking after her on Bluejay Road. Can't let myself get spooked, she thought.

All the same... "Thanks."

First stop was Zeno's All Hours Convenience, for a fresh carton of milk. Then back out into the bitter wind. Stella pulled her toque down over her ears and ducked her head and they strode along Queen Street side by side, faster and faster as the cold bit deeper. She had no breath to spare except for: "Maybe — when I get home — Molly'll be back!"

But when they reached Bluejay Road, and Stella threw open the front door, nobody answered her call.

"Mike, now I'm really getting worried!"

He stood just inside the closed door, hand on the doorknob, ready to leave. "You probably shouldn't. Odds are, everybody's all right." His eyes smiled. "I bet you wherever she is, she's with Edge."

"And that's good?"

His chin went up, his eyes cooled. "Edge is okay. He's done some stupid stuff, sure. But, you know what? It's only since Molly came to Glimmer last year that he started getting... well, really strange."

She frowned at him. "Strange, how?"

"Quiet. Hardly talks, and that's not like him. It's like he's some-where else all the time. Thinking about her, maybe. Like he can't stand to be away from her."

"Sounds like love," she said, hoping to make him smile.

He shook his head. "I sometimes wondered... well, all this Wic-can stuff..." He waved a hand at the archway and the shop beyond, with its charms and crystals. "Hey, maybe she really is a witch."

"What!"

"No kidding. It's like she's put some mojo on him. Some spell."

"Horse feathers! Molly isn't a witch any more than I am! She just likes to pretend."

"Then what happened to Edge?" He took a step forward. "Stella, he *changed*. Like he isn't my brother anymore. Like he's somebody else. Just since she came."

She rubbed her eyes, suddenly too tired to think straight. "We'll just have to find them and ask them, won't we?"

"Right." He opened the door, then touched her sleeve. "I'll be back in the morning. Okay? We'll plan what to do next. Where to start searching. I'm not giving up."

"Me neither."

The door closed and she leaned her head on it, thinking. Mike West, new friend or fresh complication?

There was a knock in the wood under her ear. She opened the door. "Lock up," Mike said. He added a stern nod for emphasis and pulled the door closed again.

She locked up.

STELLA CARRIED her bags up to Molly's bedroom, the one she and Molly had shared when they were kids. The big east room that had belonged to their parents had been turned into a library and crafts room — or possibly a Wiccan workshop, judging by the table, which was covered with bundles of dried herbs, open boxes of assorted bits of wood, stone, and shell, twists of brightly coloured yarn, packets of greyish or greenish powder and little jars of anonymous liquids. Maybe, Stella thought, they were desiccated eye of newt and pickled toe of frog.

The front corner bedroom over the porch, Travis's old room, was probably meant for a guest, but the bed was bare and one wall was stacked with cardboard cartons. Molly would just have to share her nest again this night.

The moment Stella set down her bags, the sixteen-plus hours of travelling and stress and worry caught up with her all at once. *Bed. And soon, or I'll fall over and conk out right here.*

She rooted out her flannelette pyjamas and red fleece robe and felted slipper-socks and put them on, because the house was as cold as she remembered, especially the uncarpeted oak floors. Then, for the fourth time since returning from the diner, she tried phoning Molly. Same result. She swore at the phone, went down to the kitchen to brew peppermint tea, and came up to stand at the bedroom window with the steaming mug in her hands.

Will the lake glimmer tonight?

She hoped it would. As a kid she'd always liked to look out, last thing before sleep, to see the lake glimmer. It wouldn't always.

"Magic!" Molly used to say. And Stella would impatiently repeat the scientific explanation, that the glimmer was just moonlight reflecting from quartz crystals in the stones of the lake bed. That was how the lake, and the town, had come by their names.

She'd never admitted to Molly that to her, too, it seemed a magical thing. The sight of it always made her heart dance.

Tonight the frozen lake was dark, patched with ghostly white where the wind-blown snow had gathered in drifts. A distant gleam caught her eye: a cluster of coloured lights on the far side of the lake. She turned off the bedside lamp and came back to the window. It must be some building right on the shore, all decked out for Christmas.

She stared, wondering what it was, then suddenly remembered. The old ruined pavilion used to stand in that spot. Bonnie had said the town was having it rebuilt, restored just as it used to be. Molly'd had some objection.

Stella couldn't imagine why Molly would object. The picture on the card looked gorgeous. Even as just an outline of lights it was beautiful, like a gemmed bracelet dropped in the lap of night. The sight of it lifted her heart.

Someone must be working late, getting the place ready for the party. As she watched, the lights winked out. The shore went dark. *Closing up for the night.*

Now the only lights to be seen were a car's headlights bouncing along bumpy Shore Road on the far side of the lake. Then they, too, were gone.

And gone was the brief lift of gladness. Standing by the window in the dark, Stella felt again what she'd felt in the upstairs hall a couple of hours ago. A feeling of something wrong. Suddenly the uncurtained window was like a spying eye.

She pulled the curtains closed. Something small and prickly fell from above and hit her on the nose. She jumped back. Hoping it wasn't anything alive, she went and turned on the lamp. Then picked the thing up off the floor and turned it over in her fingers.

"What in the world?"

It was a tiny bouquet the size of her thumb. Most of it was dried herbs, some plant she didn't recognize with greenish leaves and faded yellow flowers. A matchstick-sized piece of wood and an ordinary steel nail were tied up with the herb, wrapped with a strand of scarlet embroidery floss. A small bead of what looked like amber was threaded on the floss.

"Whoah!" Stella wrinkled her nose. At least this solved the mystery of the strong, almost turpentiny odour that had been bothering her. This was the source. And she was pretty sure what this thing was, too.

Magic. Charms to protect the house against ghoulies and ghosties. Oh, Molly. No wonder people think you're flaky!

But surely that one little sprig couldn't be responsible for the smell throughout the house? Stella went hunting. Ten minutes later she stood in the kitchen, shaking her head in wonder. Molly had tacked the tiny red-wrapped herbal charms over all the doors and windows. Three were fastened around the fireplace in the east wall of the shop. There was even one on the hatch to the old coal chute in the cellar.

"Well..." Stella rubbed her eyes and yawned. "Can't do any harm, I guess. Anyway, this *is* Molly's house. She can hang entire trees from the ceiling if she wants."

The ones in the bedroom, though: those could come down until Molly got back. "No way I'll breathe that stink all night!"

It took a while to find all the charms in the bedroom. There were no fewer than five. One each above the door, the window, and the bureau mirror (*For heaven's sake, Molly!*), one taped behind the headboard of the double bed, and one tucked between the mattress and the box spring. She took down the one above the balcony door in the hall, as well.

There were no plastic bags to be found in the kitchen, so Stella put the charms into an empty almond butter jar and shut the jar in a cupboard.

It took a lot of scrubbing to get the odour of the herbs off her hands. She could still smell it, faintly, when she settled to sleep.

STELLA! Stella, wake up! You must wake up!

She came wide awake in the dark, not sure why in the first confused moment. *Oh... right. A dream.* There had been a pillar-shaped cloud of golden light, and someone had been calling her. Weird!

She pushed herself up on one elbow and shivered. The room smelled like snow. A cold draft blew across her face. It felt like somebody had opened a window.

Or a door. The door to the little balcony. She'd checked the locks on the other doors, but not that one, because who could get in that way? Maybe Molly hadn't latched it properly. Maybe the wind blew it open.

Still half asleep, Stella tried to work up the will to get out of her warm bed and set foot on the icy floor. She really wanted just to burrow deep and drift....

There was a sound. A footstep. Close by.

Someone was in the room.

Chapter 5

STELLA LAY with her heart thundering in her ears. Someone or something pattered across the hardwood floor. No: a clicking rather than a pattering, suggesting hard toenails and more than two feet. The bedroom door creaked.

When her heartbeat had calmed a little and she'd caught her breath, she sat up, trying not to let the springs creak. Then, without turning on the bedside lamp, she slid out of bed and tiptoed to the door. A cold draft flowed across the floor.

She looked out into the hall. It was lighter here. A corner of Molly's medallion quilt was flipping in the icy breeze. The balcony door stood wide open. A bar of moonlight stretched from the door along the carpet runner.

Her breath drifted in the air like fog. Except for the quilt, nothing else moved. Nothing made a sound.

Then a shape slid into the shaft of moonlight. The silver shaft cut the shape in half. One side remained in shadow, dark on dark. The other stood out vividly, like a picture painted in daubs of white on black paper.

Something like a dog. It was no colour in the silver light, but more pale than dark. Half crouched, a long narrow head low between hunched shoulders, sharp muzzle thrust forward, long pointed ears laid back along the flat skull. Jaws slightly open. A hint of teeth.

A dog in the house. Stella stood frozen in the bedroom doorway. A dog, or something like a dog, that must have jumped to the second-floor balcony and pushed open the door and then walked around her bedroom in the middle of the night. What kind of a dog could do that?

It wasn't looking at her. It stood still as ice. Its breath made no cloud in the moonlit air. Her hand rose all by itself to clasp her star pendant. At the movement, the narrow head turned. It looked at her now and its eyes flashed: two moon-pale greenish glints, like a cat's eyes at night.

It moved no more than that. It saw her and just looked. Not scared at all.

She stared back, breath caught, her hand so tight on the star that the points dug into her fingers. Then the dog, if it was a dog, turned away and padded, silent on carpet, through the balcony doorway and out of sight.

Reaction set in. Trembling all over, Stella leaned against the wall and started to ooze down toward the floor. Then jerked herself up-right. Gulped air, dashed along the hall, slammed the balcony door and threw her weight against it.

She pawed at the lock. There was a key in it, one of the old-fashioned brass ones that dated from when the house was built, in the 1940s.

Where was the dog-thing now? Keeping one hand on the key, Stella opened the door a crack and peeked through. There was noth-ing on the balcony. She pulled the door wide. The half-circle of the balcony floor was dusted lightly with snow, but none was falling now. There should be footprints. Stella blinked up at the moon, then down at the balcony floor. No footprints.

Okay, so it jumped.

Keeping her feet inside the door, she set her hands on the iron railing and leaned out until she could see the ground. Nothing down there but moonlit snow. Hard to tell if there were any footprints. But

it wouldn't be too far to drop from here, and the critter could probably jump that railing. It was not impossible.

Still, it ought to be too high to jump *up* here from the ground, if
you had no hands to grab with. There was a shed among the big pines
at the end of the yard, close to the lake, where Molly kept her bike-
and-trailer ("I'll get a car when I can afford a nice non-polluting
electric."), but that was too far off to be any help getting to or from
the balcony.

She pushed herself back inside, closed the door, and turned the
key with cold-numbed hands. The rest of the night she dozed and
waked a dozen times.

NEXT MORNING, the first thing Stella did on waking was to pull
her phone out from under the pillow and try Molly's number. Still no
good.

She dressed in jeans and jersey and sweater, ran down and put on
her coat and boots and let herself out the kitchen door into the back
yard. There had been no more snow in the night, a glance out at the
little balcony had showed that.

The back yard was a sheet of pure, perfect white sweeping down
to the shed and the row of pines. There were tracks in the snow here,
plenty of them. Bird tracks, rabbit tracks, deer tracks, tomcat tracks.

But none of them human. And none that seemed to fit with what
she'd seen of that dog, or coyote, or whatever it was. And no sign
that anything had dropped from the balcony.

Dream? Stella blew out a plume of icy breath. *Must have been.*
Strange how she had to keep telling herself that. What a bizarre
dream, and so vivid!

A sound: a clink on glass. She spun around and there was a face
at the kitchen window. Her heart thumped. And then she threw out

her arms and shouted: "Molly!"

The back door flew open. Molly burst out, laughing and crying, her cardinal-red parka flapping, and threw herself into Stella's arms.

"YOUR PENDANT! Your pendant — it's safe?" It was the first clear thing Molly said, after minutes of babbling.

Stella put an arm around her and urged her toward the door. "Sure, it's safe. Molly, are you all right? What happened to you? I've been phoning and phoning! Where've you been?"

"Never mind that now! I need to know your pendant's safe."

"Oh, okay! But why..." Stella reached into the collar of her sweater. Molly batted her hand down.

"Not here! Inside!" She grabbed Stella by the arm. "It might be watching!"

"It? What?"

"Let's just get inside!"

Back in the kitchen, Molly made sure the door was locked. Then she had to see Stella's star pendant and touch it. Finally she collapsed into a chair by the wicker table, pulled up her knees inside clasped arms and huddled in her parka.

"Molly!" Stella knelt in front of her and took her hands. They were icy. She pressed them between her own and gave them a shake. "Molly, are you hurt? What happened? Tell me!"

Molly blinked at her from under a tangle of brown curls. "I'm not sure you'd believe me. You're such a sceptic."

"Try me."

"Okay." She took a deep breath. "I was with Edge."

Edge. Wild West. "What did he do? Did he hurt you?" Stella's grip tightened.

"No! Edge never — I mean, not when he's himself, he wouldn't.

But he wanted my moon pendant. Only he didn't really. It was s-something else that wanted it."

"Something else? Molly, what the hell are you talking about?"

"I never did see it clearly, just hints and glimpses. It looked sort of like—"

Knuckles rapped on the kitchen window. Molly yelped and jumped from her chair, hands at her mouth. A face looked in through the glass.

"It's all right! It's only Mike."

"Oh, Mike." Molly dropped her hands and sank back into the chair. "All right, let him in. He'll need to hear this too."

Chapter 6

"WHERE'S Edge?"

"Boots, Mike." Stella pointed him at the rubber boot tray near the door, watched him kick off his snowy boots, then steered him into the second chair at the kitchen table.

"Where—"

"Can't you see she's too upset to think? Now sit, both of you, while I make coffee. We all need it."

"Tea." Molly pointed at the cupboard over the stove. "It's all I've got. Coffee's poison."

After tea was brewed the story came out in scraps and patches.

"It was Sunday afternoon," Molly began. "Edge came in his pickup to drive me to the new pavilion. He'd been working on it, helping to restore it, even though I'd told him over and over how dangerous that was."

"Dangerous?" Stella lifted the teapot above Molly's cup. "Why?"

Molly opened her mouth to answer, but Mike put a hand up. "All that creepy stuff about the pavilion — please — later. Right now I just want to know about Edge."

"Well, he wanted to show me the building, what a good job they were doing. He was so pleased about it. Almost his old self. He'd been so ... dark ... lately." Molly frowned and shook her head. "So I went with him."

"You left your bag behind. All your ID. Scared me to death!"

"Sorry. He was in a hurry, said we'd just be half an hour and then he'd have me right back. So I jumped in the truck and off we went."

Only, they hadn't stopped at the pavilion. Edge had driven past it, along the lake's north shore, then up into the hills. "I lost track of where we went. It got dark, the roads all look the same up there, nothing but snow and trees. I asked him where we were going, and he just mumbled something. I told him I wanted to go home, and he didn't answer. Didn't look at me. Except once, and then I.... " Molly's voice wobbled. "I didn't know who he was."

Stella reached across the table and covered Molly's shaking hands.

"What the hell does that mean?" Mike's hands curled into fists.

"He was someone else. Somebody I didn't recognize."

"Someone else? You mean—"

Stella shot him a look. "Let her talk!" To Molly she said: "Couldn't you have phoned? You had your phone with you, right? It wasn't in your bag."

"Yeah, I had it in my jacket pocket and pulled it out but it, um, it escaped."

They both looked at her.

"The window was half open beside me. The phone popped out of my hand and flew out the window. Lord knows where it is now."

"Funny," Stella said.

"Yeah. So then I made up my mind to escape myself." Molly had waited until the truck slowed down on a bend, then tried to open the door and jump out. She got it open, but it slammed shut — "like somebody pushed it from outside, only there wasn't anybody, at least I didn't *see* anybody" — and Edge ran the windows up and locked all the doors.

After hours of driving they reached a clearing in the woods, with a small log cabin. "More like a shack," Molly said. "Just the one room, and an outhouse out back. Wood stove in the corner, lots of firewood stacked. No idea who it belongs to. I lit the stove, so we were warm. There was an old sofa that I think mice had been nesting in, and a cupboard with some canned soup, and that was it."

"Oh, Molly!" Stella bounced out of her chair. "You must be starving! I'll make—"

"No, sit back down. I couldn't eat. Not yet."

"Edge," Mike prompted.

"Did he hurt you?" Stella demanded.

"No!" Molly shook her tangled head. "He wouldn't, I swear!"

Stella went to the cupboard and poked around for something to feed Molly. "So, what did he do?"

"I asked him what he wanted, and he just said 'The moon.' I didn't understand. Then he pointed at my pendant." She touched the front of her sweater.

"What pendant?" Mike frowned. "This makes no sense."

"It's a crescent-shaped gold pendant she wears. But why would he want that?"

"I've got a theory. I'll explain later." Molly drained her cup. "The thing is, he kept trying to take it from me, but he never could."

"Who stopped him?" Mike looked incredulous. "You?"

"No. He stopped himself. He kept walking around and around me, reaching for it, then pulling his hand back. He kept muttering at himself to *take it*, then he'd snap at himself, *No!* I fell asleep on the sofa and when I woke up it was morning and he was still there, staring at me, muttering, back and forth: it was like he was arguing with somebody. Somebody I couldn't see. And he never did take my pendant."

"Poor Edge." Mike pushed his untasted cup away. "He's really lost it now."

"I don't think so." Molly touched his wrist. "Not crazy."

"What d'you think's wrong with him, then?"

"I think he's possessed," Molly said calmly.

"Possessed!" Stella spilled half a package of Flax 'n' Hemp cereal over the counter. Mike goggled, then rolled his eyes up at the ceiling.

"Yes, and I think I know what by. I could almost see it. Once I did, sort of, just a flicker, out of the corner of my eye."

"Molly! Talk sense, please. You saw what?"

"The thing he was arguing with. The thing that's been shadowing him, darkening him, these last few weeks. The thing that really wanted my pendant. I bet you've seen it too, Mike."

"Don't know what you're talking about." Mike turned his head away.

With daylight, Molly had looked for a chance to escape. But Edge never let her out of his sight, not once. And he never seemed to sleep. "It went on like that all day, and all the next night and day. You must've been here by then, Stella."

"Yes, and Mike and I went to the police! We've got your photo circulating across half the province!"

Molly laughed. "Cool! I'm famous!"

"Infamous," Stella said. "How did you get away, finally?"

"Edge got more and more into sitting by the wall, staring at me, muttering. I began to think he really didn't see me, he was so tied up in this argument he was having. So I sort of drifted toward the door. He didn't notice, he didn't stop me. I was almost there when I saw what was guarding it. I'd been getting glimpses of this… thing … near Edge. At his heels, under his elbow. Now, suddenly, it was at the door. The shadow." Molly drew a shaky breath. "I couldn't pass it. It scared the daylights out of me. And then it, it s-started to come toward me."

"Easy!" Stella said. "You need to lie down."

"Not yet! Listen. That was when Edge woke up. I think it was because the thing was threatening me. He made a huge rush at the door, shouting and waving his arms, like he was fighting something off. He burst open the door and yelled at me — *Get out, run, go!* And I did."

"When was this?" Mike stood up. "And where, exactly? Is he still in the cabin?"

"He was when I left. I just ran. It was almost dawn, this morning. Mike, I have no idea where the cabin is." Molly met his frown. "I don't! I only know it isn't really all that far up in the hills. We must have driven in circles to get there. When there was enough light, I saw the lake below, through the trees. I found the county road, hitched a ride on a farm truck, and here I am."

"But why?" Stella set another cup of tea in front of Molly, and a bowl of Flax 'n' Hemp cereal with milk. "Why would Edge kidnap you?"

"I told you: my pendant. He wants it. Which means he, I mean *it*, probably wants yours as well." Molly pulled a fine gold chain from her collar.

Stella pulled out hers too, unfastened the chain, and held her pendant beside Molly's. Seen together, it was obvious they were a set. Molly's was a small crescent moon the size of her thumbnail, worked in gold, with a tiny diamond set in the centre. Stella's was its mate, right down to the diamond, except hers was shaped like a star. Both had been pierced at one end, to allow a jump ring to go through.

Mike bent to see. He sat back. "I don't get it."

Molly grinned. "Remember when we got these, Stella-Star?"

Stella had to smile at the old nickname. "I was twelve, and Molly was thirteen," she told Mike. "Our Great-Grandmother Lily left me the pendants in her will — she died a bit after I was born, really old, over ninety. They looked like earrings without hooks. But it didn't seem fair that Lily left nothing at all to Molly, so I broke up the set. I took the star because I'm Stella, which means star, and Molly took the moon."

"Because Molly means moon?" Mike was blandly polite.

"No, because the moon is the sign of the Goddess," Molly said solemnly.

He studied the ceiling. "Uh-huh."

"Ever since, I've always worn my star." Stella laughed as she fastened the chain around her neck again. "I call it my good luck piece. Which is funny, because I don't believe in luck."

"Well, you'd better start believing." Molly pushed back her chair and got up. "You'd better start asking yourself why Great-Gran Lily left the pair to you and not to me. Before anything else happens."

"All right, why did she?"

"Because you're the one who has her gift. The Sight. She must have known that as soon as you were born. I wish we had that letter of hers that came with the pendants. Remember?"

"Letter." Stella vaguely recalled it. "The one Travis wouldn't let me read? No idea where it is."

"I don't have time for this." Mike crossed to the kitchen door and started pulling on his boots.

Molly followed him. "Where are you going?"

"Where d'you think? To find Edge."

"Don't go yet. You don't know—"

"I don't need to know." He straightened up and gave her a bleak stare. "You're going to report this to the cops, aren't you? You're going to have Edge arrested."

"Of course he should be arrested!" Stella flared. "He kidnapped her!"

"No." Molly shook her head.

"No? But, Molly—"

"He's not himself, I told you. This was not his fault." She met Mike's eyes and nodded gravely. "I'll do everything in my power to rescue him. That's a promise."

Mike ducked his head. "I think you mean that. But, like I told Stella last night, it's only since you came to town that he changed. If he went off the deep end, it's because of you." He grabbed the doorknob.

Molly put a hand on his arm. "It's only since the *pendant* came to town that he changed. You see? There's something here that wants the pendant. Something has got at Edge. Got *in* him. That's what I meant by possessed. You've seen it too, don't pretend you haven't."

"Seen what?" Stella asked, at her shoulder.

"Well, I didn't get a real good look." Molly shivered. "But in that shack, that time by the door, I thought it looked something like a dog."

"A dog?" Stella repeated. *My dream.*

Mike expression was so blank he might as well have been shouting.

"Right, only not your average lovable mutt. It looked sort of wild, sort of like..." Molly spread her hands and waved them. "Like a coyote or wolf. But not even as normal as that. I mean, it seemed too, well, *focussed.*"

Mike pulled the door open. "I don't care what's got at him. I'm going to find him and bring him home before he gets in more trouble. Or freezes to death."

Chapter 7

MIKE HAD ARRIVED on a snowmobile and had parked it on the front walk. Stella and Molly went into the shop and watched through a window as he kicked the sled into life and buzzed away up the street toward the trail that circled the lake.

"We should've gone with him," Molly said. "We should be helping him search."

"We'd only slow him down." Stella tapped Molly on the shoulder. "What you need now is bed. Sleep. Recharge the batteries."

"My batteries are just fine, thanks!" Molly looked around the store. "What time is it? Eight-thirty?" She clapped hands to head. "Yowsers, I open at nine!"

"Open the store? After all you've been through? Molly—"

"Yes!" Molly whirled to face her, suddenly fierce. "Stella, I need to get back to normal. I'm too weirded out to sleep, anyway. And if I did sleep, I'd have nightmares." She scurried out of the room. "Got to wash and change quick!" she called over her shoulder.

Brisk footsteps ran up the stairs, then along the upstairs hall. They skidded to a stop. Then came a shriek. "Stella!"

When Stella burst breathlessly into the back bedroom she found Molly standing with her hands on her hips, glaring around.

"What? What?"

Molly pointed an accusing finger. "What happened to all my protective charms?"

"Oh, for crumbs sake! I thought something was wrong!" Stella sank onto the bed. "Your charms? I took them down — No, don't blow up! Not all of them. Just the ones in this room. Oh, and the one above the balcony door. I couldn't sleep with that smell."

Molly shook her fists at the ceiling. "Disaster! Where are they?"

"Br-rother!" Stella ran downstairs to the kitchen and was up again a minute later, carrying the jar. "Why couldn't you have made them out of something that smells nice, like lavender? Then I would've left them alone."

Molly shook the sprigs out onto the bed. She was smiling, her anger swiftly gone. "That's St. John's wort, that herb with the yellow flowers." She touched it gently. "It keeps hostile influences out of the house. The wood is ash: strong against evil."

"Hm," Stella said noncommittally. "And what's the nail there for?"

"The nail is steel, and of course any iron or steel wards off the forces of darkness."

"The forces of darkness. Right." Stella studied the sprig. "What's that bead?"

"Amber. It guards against the evil eye. Don't sneer, kid. And the red thread — red, the colour of life — binds the charm and makes it stronger." Molly nodded as if what she'd said made perfect sense.

"O-*kay*. And you believe this?"

"I believe in keeping an open mind." Molly tapped her on the forehead. "Which is more than I can say for some people. Now you, dearest sister, are going to help me put them all up again."

It was while they were folding up the stepladder, fifteen minutes later, that Molly said casually: "So, when did you see that dog?"

"Uh." Stella nearly dropped the tack hammer on her foot. "What dog?"

"Come on. You just about jumped out of your skin when I mentioned it. Mike, too, in his keep-it-all-inside way. You've both seen it.

Tell!"

"All right. It was last night." Stella described her dream, the sense of being called, the fading golden presence. Then waking, the sound of dog footsteps, and her sight of the wild-looking something-like-a-dog in the hallway.

"Hm." Molly studied her thoughtfully. "Interesting that you saw it so clearly, when all I got was a glimpse."

"But of course I never really *saw* it. When I thought I woke up, before, that had to be part of the dream."

"Why so sure?"

"Obvious. If it were real, there would've been footprints in the snow."

"You think?" Molly rubbed her arms as if they were cold. "The dog I saw wouldn't have left footprints, I bet, but it was real enough. And I was wide awake."

"I'm not so sure of that, but let it go. I guess you're going to say it was lusting after my star pendant."

"Yes! And the only reason it was able to get into the house was because you'd made a breach in the protection, by taking down my bundles. Promise me you won't do that again!"

"All right, take it easy, I won't." Stella grinned. "Any idea what a dog would want with little gold pendants? To wear on his collar, maybe?"

"Stel, you know as well as I do: that thing's not just a dog. It's something else."

"Like what?"

"Don't know yet. Gotta rush!" Molly dashed into the washroom.

Stella carried the stepladder downstairs to the kitchen and put it away in the broom closet. Ten minutes later, Molly reached into the front window of the shop and flipped over the SORRY, WE'RE

CLOSED sign to show the side that said YES! WE'RE OPEN.

Stella picked up an anti-static duster and started flicking at a display of paperweights disguised as crystal balls. "Look, even if you grant that there are these powers of darkness, and I'm not sure I do, there still has to be some logic to what's happening, right? Some reason behind it all. Why would these dark powers suddenly take an interest in Great-Gran Lily's pendants?"

"Because, obviously, they are magical objects. Important ones. And I brought mine back to Glimmer, and that's when the weird stuff started, according to Mike. So the dark powers must be here." Molly opened the cash box under the terminal and calmly began sorting through it. "Lily was certainly a white witch, just like me." She sighed. "I mean, not just like me. She was a lot stronger."

Stella had always thought the colourful stories about Great-Grandmother Lily Craig Macmillan were just that: stories to be passed on and enjoyed, but not taken seriously. They said she had Second Sight, the mysterious ability to see hidden things that ran in Scottish families (according to the folklore), most often in the women.

Lily always knew when someone was about to die, it was said. She knew whether an expected baby would be a boy or a girl, no ultrasound needed. She knew when one of her grandchildren or great-grandchildren, thousands of miles away on the other side of the continent, was having a really bad day and needed a phone call.

"Molly," Stella began. "You don't seriously believe..."

"Of course I do!" Molly walked over to the big mirror near her display of fair trade shawls, tucked a saffron-coloured silk shirt more securely into tight jeans, and artistically mussed her dangling ringlets. "And I have it too: Lily's gift, I mean. I have just enough of it to know that I don't have very much." She whirled and stabbed a finger at Stella. "And *you* have it coming out your ears!"

Before Stella could protest, the door swung open. The day's first customer stepped in, stamping snow off his boots: a small, bouncy man with eager eyes.

"Molly! You're back! Where have you been?"

"Well hello, Mr. Savas. Yes, I've been away. Business, you know."

"And Edge is back too, is he?"

"I've no idea." Molly widened her eyes. "Why, did he go somewhere?"

After Mr. Savas left (without buying anything), Molly laughed. "Now everybody will know I'm back. That man is the worst gossip in the county."

"Oops, that reminds me. You'd better call Travis, so he won't worry. And call the OPP, to let them know you're not missing."

"Travis wouldn't worry if he heard I'd fallen into a volcano. 'Isn't that just like Molly,' he'd say. And *you* can call the OPP. It was you who went to them in the first place."

Stella phoned them both, using the land line. The call to the police was embarrassing. The call to Travis was irritating on both sides. It was only 6:30 a.m. in Nanaimo and she'd interrupted him in the middle of shaving. Stella hung up with a bang. "I don't know why I bother!"

Chapter 8

MAGIC BY THE LAKE did brisk business all morning. It was obvious, more or less, that some of the customers had come in just to ask Molly where she'd been, and with whom. Molly smiled charmingly and told them nothing much.

Most of them bought something before they left. The crystal Christmas tree ornaments sold out. Pillow sachets and herbal potpourris went fast; so did the shawls and the silver and amber jewellery, bought for gift-giving.

In the early afternoon a tall, cheerful-looking redheaded woman came in. "I've come to make you change your mind," she called out, still in the doorway.

"That's not going to happen, Joyce. Sorry!" Molly pulled Stella over to be introduced.

Joyce's blue eyes gleamed at Stella. "Maybe you can talk your sister into giving me a hand. I'm in charge of decorating the pavilion: for the party, you know. But with the workers still in there, we'll have only a day to do our bit. Maybe less. And Molly has a talent for making things look spiffy in a hurry. Molly, honey, you're needed!"

"Sorry. If it were anything else, I'd be right in there helping. But you know what I think about that pavilion."

Joyce laughed. "Come on! We'll have a great time and you'll miss it."

"Uh-uh. Stella and I aren't going anywhere near that party."

"Hold on just a minute!" Stella shot Molly a look. This was the first time she had thought about going to the Festival of Lights — the first time she'd had a spare moment to think about it. "Since when do you decide what parties I go to? It might be fun!"

"Oh, well. It's too late now, anyway. All the tickets have been snapped up."

"That's true. Except for...." Joyce reached into her purse and pulled out a small envelope. She waved it triumphantly. "Tickets — two pair! Lend me a hand and they're yours."

"That's cool — but no, I won't change my mind."

Joyce sighed. "Molly, this is sheer superstition!"

Molly's smile began to look forced. Stella felt an argument brewing. She'd quickly decided that she liked Joyce and didn't want Molly to quarrel with a good friend, so she moved in with a diversion.

"The pavilion: it's not finished yet? It looked so pretty when I saw it last night, across the lake, all lit up like a Christmas tree."

Joyce looked at her blankly. "That can't have been the pavilion you saw. The lights are up, but they aren't wired in yet. That's supposed to happen tomorrow."

"But there's nothing else in that spot. What else could it have been?"

"Mm… car lights, maybe? Or the moon reflecting off the ice?"

Stella shook her head. "Nothing like that. This was all colours."

"Well then, it's a mystery."

After Joyce left, no longer smiling, Stella searched through the books on sale and found a locally published history of the county. The cover showed a faded photo of the original pavilion. In the picture it was summer. The women standing under the graceful arches wore slim ankle-length skirts and tailored jackets. The men had on high white collars and flat straw hats. A paragraph on the back said:

Cover photo: The Town of Glimmer's "Party Pavilion" was built in 1897 to celebrate Queen Victoria's Diamond Jubilee. For nearly thirty years it was a popular spot for swimming, skating, picnics, and dances. The pavilion collapsed during a dance party on December 21, 1926. Tragically, many of the town's young people were killed that night, crushed under falling timbers or drowned when the currents swept them under the ice. *See page 22.*

Stella carried the book over to where Molly was re-stocking the DVDs and showed her the cover. "Is the new one really so much like the old one?"

"Yes! They're identical! That was the whole point, to restore the old pavilion down to the last detail. I went to the town council meeting and objected, but of course nobody listened."

"Well, what could you say? That you had a bad feeling about it?"

"I had dreams." Molly went on sorting the DVDs, though they didn't need it. "I dreamed that everybody died — again. No, of course I couldn't tell them that!" She laughed shortly. "I just said it was a waste of taxpayers' money."

Stella leafed through the book to page 22. Like everyone who'd ever lived in Glimmer, she knew about the disaster of 1926. There was hardly a family for miles around that hadn't lost a son or daughter that night. The collapse had never been fully explained. There had been talk of the ever-flowing springs beneath the building undermining its foundations, which then gave way under the weight of the crowd.

The brief account in the book ended with a long list of names: the victims of the Pavilion Tragedy. Stella ran her finger down it, looking for Macmillans. There weren't any, but there under the Cs was Aurora Craig, Great-Grandmother Lily's sister. Stella wondered if Lily had missed the dance that night, or if she'd been there, but had somehow escaped the collapse.

About mid-afternoon, business slowed to a trickle. At three o'clock Molly threw up her hands. "That's it! We're closing! Come on, we're going skating, just like we used to!"

"Don't you think you'd better cool it now and get some rest?"

"Absolutely not! Don't fuss, okay? I'm perfectly fine!"

Molly had bought an extra pair of skates weeks ago, for just this purpose. They bundled up, waded through the deep snow down to the lakeshore behind the house, and sat on a log on the bank to lace up their skates. Then Molly flew off like a bird. After a few clumsy steps and some teetering back and forward, Stella found her feet and flew after her.

They swept along the curving shore toward the inlet where the streams and springs that fed the lake came in. Hills around the inlet created a sheltered spot perfect for skating, with smooth ice and little wind.

There were other people here: parents with children, teens, young couples skimming hand in hand. Some had faces she vaguely remembered. Molly, who seemed to know everybody, laughingly fended off questions about herself and Edge and re-introduced Stella.

It was like a surprise holiday. The level beams of sun were bright gold, the ice dazzling. A man with a cart on the shore sold hot dogs, hot chocolate and coffee, and chemical hand warmers. Behind him, the rebuilt pavilion shone bright and new, its white paint gleaming, its tall windows glittering.

Stella left Molly talking with her friends and skated out on the lake, farther and farther, until the laughter and shouts of the skaters melted into the whistle of the wind. In every direction the shore looked far away, the sky immense.

She remembered skating here, as a child. On a bright day you could see a long way down into the clear ice. Bits of leaves and twigs were suspended in it, like vegetables in aspic.

She shivered suddenly. People used to say that some nights, when the moon was bright, you could still see the faces of the dead, the ones lost when the pavilion collapsed, beneath the ice.

Some even said that was why the lake glimmered. It was the eyes of the dead, looking up at the moon.

She shook her head and laughed. People would say anything! Of course there were no dead people in the lake.

But what was that? She spotted a blur of colour under the ice a few yards away. *A lost scarf, or a mitten.* She skated over to investigate. *Definitely something here.*

She bent down and found herself looking at a girl's face.

Chapter 9

STELLA FROZE, bent over, stiff with shock.

A girl. A dead girl. Young. Sixteen, seventeen? The face was frost-white. Pale gold hair stood out in frozen waves around the head. There was something strange about the clothing, but Stella only had time to file away the details in the back of her mind, no time to think about them.

The eyes opened and gazed up at her.

Oh my God!

Not dead. Trapped. The eyes were sky-blue and terrified. Desperate.

Stella fell to her knees and pawed uselessly at the ice. The girl's left hand moved up across her body as if to scratch at the under surface. Something gold gleamed on her wrist.

Trapped, drowning. "No!" Stella pulled her feet around in front of her and used the heel of her skate blade like a pick, gouging the ice. Frozen fragments showered up, but the thick ice would not crack.

The girl's mouth moved, mouthing at her — nothing she could make out. The arm moved again. The left wrist turned, the gold object gleamed.

"I'll get help! Hold on!" she yelled, as if the girl could hear her. She scrambled up, slithered and fell full length, scrambled up again, and skated, head down, legs flailing, back toward the inlet.

Her shouts brought the other skaters. They followed her back to the spot. It was easy to find, the place where her skate blades had gouged shallow holes in the ice.

The girl was gone.

Drowned. I let her drown.

"Stella. Stel! Look at me." It was Molly. Stella blinked at her through tears. "Maybe she moved," Molly said urgently. "Maybe the currents moved her. Let's look."

They searched the ice for yards around, but found nothing. Most of the skaters shook their heads and drifted back toward the inlet. "Wait! Where are you going?" Stella called. "We have to find her! Come back!" None of them came back.

She knelt on the ice again and tried to see past the bits of debris and tiny bubbles into the dark water beneath, searching for a glimpse of white that might be a face. There was nothing.

Those sky-blue eyes closed forever. That white face, sinking down into the icy darkness.

Molly crouched beside her and wrapped an arm around her. "We should go home and think about this."

"Think? Molly! We've got to *do* something!"

"But, Stel—"

"A girl drowned! We've got to call the police, the paramedics!"

"Wouldn't do a damn bit of good," said a new voice behind them.

The only onlooker left was a tall, bony, white-bearded man wearing boots, not skates. He had a face rugged as granite. "Oh, um, hi," Molly said. She looked nervous. "Stel, it's Ken Lennox. Edge's boss. At least, I think he's still Edge's boss."

"Don't worry, I'm still his boss. If he ever comes back to work." The old man let go a brief, bleak smile.

Stella beat her hands on the ice. "Why the hell are we bothering with introductions when a girl just *drowned?*" She lurched to her feet. "There could still be time, if we move fast, if we find her. We could still save her. Let's *go!*"

"Calm down, young lady." He patted her shoulder awkwardly. "Whatever you saw has been there for near ninety years. There's no saving it now."

"That's a load of—" She fought down anger. "I did see her! She was there!" She stabbed at the ice with a mittened hand. "She looked at me, she opened her eyes, she tried to talk to me!"

"Now, how could that be? How could she've been trying to talk from under the ice?"

"Well, she…" Stella stumbled to a halt. The strangeness of it hit her.

"And think of this," said Mr. Lennox. "There's no sign of any break in the ice, not nearby. She didn't just fall through. To get to this spot she must've travelled a long way. Under the ice. In that water. How long d'you think a person lasts in water that cold?"

Not very long, Stella guessed. After a long moment, while Molly held her hand tight, she said quietly: "I did see her."

"I don't doubt it. You're not the first to see her, or others like her."

"But—"

"I mean the dead. The dead under the ice. Not the actual bodies, they're gone, buried. Just whatever's hung around from that time."

"From when the pavilion collapsed," Molly said.

"Right. From all those years ago. Like some of them can't leave."

Stella shuddered with sudden cold. "Might as well get home," she muttered.

"Just one thought." The old man held her eyes. "People say things have never been good for this town since that day in '26. All those young people killed, it took the heart right out of us. But just in the last few years, we're starting to put the past behind us. That means we don't spread stories about ghosts in the lake. And we'd take it as a kindness if you kept whatever you saw to yourself."

THE SUN had edged down behind the hills by the time they set off for home. The sky in the west turned a glowing apple-green. Golden lights bloomed along the shore. They were nearly home when Stella dug in her blades and swooped to a stop. She spun to look back over the frozen lake.

Molly slid up beside her. "Baby sister, give in. Admit it. You saw a ghost."

"I don't believe in ghosts!"

"What, still? Then what was it?"

Stella shrugged her shoulders irritably.

"Come on, let's have it." Molly took her arm. "Tell me about it. Describe this girl."

Stella dug the details out of memory as they glided slowly along the shore. The sapphire-blue eyes, fringed with black lashes. The face, a perfect oval. Full, pink mouth. Hair a halo of gold. "She was really pretty. No, more. She was beautiful."

"What was she wearing, did you see?"

They sat on the log to unlace their skates and pull their boots back on. "Something peach-coloured." Stella thought back. "Silky, the way it moved in the water. Kind of skimpy too, now I think about it. Not short but thin. A dress, not a coat. Her arms were bare."

"Not exactly ice-skating gear."

"And there was something else." Stella groped for the detail as they walked back to the house. "She had on some kind of bracelet, gold. It was on her left wrist. I can't recall any more than that."

"Sounds to me," Molly said, as they filed in through the kitchen door, "like your ghost was a real party girl. Silk dress, gold jewellery.

Way cool!"

Party girl, Stella thought. The party of December 21, 1926. She shook her head hard.

As soon as her boots were off, Molly phoned Mike to ask about Edge. There was no answer. "He must still be out searching."

They made up the spare bedroom for Stella, who thought of Mike out there in the cold, doggedly patrolling the back roads. To keep busy and occupy her mind, she walked to the grocery store on Queen Street and bought food: butter, bread, cheese, eggs, bacon, coffee, more milk, and eggnog. She detoured to the LCBO for a mickey of rum, fairly sure that Molly wouldn't have any.

After supper (toasted omelet sandwich for Stella, tofu scramble for Molly) they did the dishes together the way they used to when they were younger: Molly washing, Stella drying, and the two of them singing together at the top of their lungs.

"That was awesome!" Molly curled up on the sofa in the shop facing the fireplace. "*The Shepherd* is on CBC Radio at eight. That Christmas story narrated by Alan Maitland, remember? It's a ghost story too, come to think of it. We'll listen together, okay? With eggnog!" She yawned hugely. "But first I'll just rest my eyes. Give me half an hour."

"It's cold in here. I'll get blankets." Stella went upstairs to get the extra blanket from her own room, then the one on Molly's bed. She didn't turn on any lights. Turning from the bed she glanced out the window, stopped short, and went over and stared through the glass.

The pavilion was lit up again. No mistaking that spot, and there was no other building close to it, nothing big enough to put on such a show.

But Joyce said the lights wouldn't be wired up until tomorrow. So it can't be the pavilion.

She thudded down the stairs and into the shop. "Molly, guess what!" She bit off the rest. Molly was sound asleep, her head nestled into the corner of the sofa, mouth slightly open.

Stella tucked blankets around her and let her sleep. Then went and looked out the kitchen window. Even from this level she could see the lights on the far shore, blue and gold and ruby twinkling though the trees.

This is getting to be a pain in the neck!

First the doggish creature that was or was not a dream. Then the girl under the ice who was or was not a ghost. And now the lit-up pavilion that was or was not a mirage.

Stella was used to trusting her senses. She was used to things *making* sense. She was tired of having to doubt her own eyes.

It's going to drive me crazy if this keeps up. I need to know what's going on!

Chapter 10

THE NIGHT was clear, the moon bright. As Stella stepped out from under the trees at the edge of Glimmer Lake the sky seemed to expand, as if someone had lifted a giant lid off the earth and let in the light of heaven. Outside the dark halo of the moon, the stars crackled blue and gold and white.

Drawing a deep breath of frosty air, she set off across the ice, taking the faraway coloured lights for a guide. The lake glimmered faintly. In places snow had been blown into thin-packed drifts that squeaked underfoot. Farther out, where wind had swept the ice clean, she slid her feet along like a skater. She never looked back, never took her eyes from the lights on the far shore.

Step after step, the lights grew nearer, clearer. The shape of the pavilion showed unmistakably, the curved roof and arches outlined in jewel-like sparkles that reflected in the glassy ice ahead.

Nearer, nearer, and now there was music. Only a whisper at first, so faint she had to pull the toque away from her ears to be sure it wasn't just the wind. No, it was music all right, and there was melody, a tune she almost recognized.

Wait, was that …. Yes! The band was playing *Bye Bye Blackbird.*

The music grew louder as she walked. The beat was quick, light-hearted …... *Make my bed, light the light, I'll be home late tonight...* In 1926, that must have been brand new.

Nearer. Now she could see people through the tall arched windows. Dancers bobbing and whirling past. Men in formal black and white. Women in silky knee-length dresses coloured amber and ivory and rose, and sparkling bands in their hair. Faces that smiled and laughed. Stella thought she would know them if she saw them again.

Now she was standing on the ice five or six long strides from where the pavilion's wraparound deck jutted out from the shore. The music played, the people danced and laughed, the lights sparkled.

And then, as she watched, it all stopped. The music cut out so suddenly it left a ringing in her ears. The dancers froze in place. The lights went out.

When the purple after-images cleared from her vision, there was only the moonlight, the silvery lake and snowy shore, and the pavilion, a cage for nothing but darkness.

STELLA CROSSED the last few metres to the shore. The pavilion was built out over the ice on five of its six sides. In summer it would perch like a houseboat on the water. A wide wooden deck ran around the outside and joined the building to the shore on its sixth side.

She walked around the deck, looking in. It was hard to see anything past the moon-reflecting glass. Then a surprise. A door, mostly glass like the windows, moved under her hand. She pulled it open, stepped inside, and closed it behind her.

Moonlight slanted in and showed a big, bare hall with a gleaming wooden floor and windows everywhere. It smelled of newly sawn wood and fresh paint. Brass gleamed in one corner: the bar, Stella guessed. Little white tables, stacked with upended spindly chairs, stood along one side.

Black cords dangled and looped from the ceiling beams: the unfinished wiring. The hall didn't look anywhere near ready for the party on Saturday, only three days away.

It didn't look as if it had been full of dancers just a minute ago, either.

"Okay," Stella said quietly, "I guess I believe in ghosts now. Because I sure didn't imagine that."

A time slip, she thought. A small cosmic mistake. Was it possible? Maybe that's what ghosts were: people accidentally shifted from their time to ours, just for a moment. With a little work she could believe that.

She stood looking around the silent, new-smelling hall. *Well, their moment is over. I've seen them. Maybe I'll never see them again.* She wasn't sure if she felt glad or sad about that.

She turned to leave. Then turned back again as something bright caught her eye. A small object hung in the centre of the space at about the height of her head. It shifted and winked as it caught the moonlight.

Walking closer, she saw a tiny golden shape turning slowly, first this way, then that, as if it hung from the ceiling on an invisible string.

She looked up. Her breath went out in a cloud of vapour.

There was no string. There was no ceiling. Only the glitter of stars. The little golden shape reflected spangles of light over broken timbers crusted with ice. The floor crunched under her boot soles. She looked down and saw cracked boards, furry with frost. Jagged holes showed black water glinting below.

There was just enough of the walls left to show that this was the pavilion: the original. And that something terrible had happened here.

Stella took two more careful steps. Now she was close enough to see the shape of the little gold thing that hung in mid-air all by itself. A sun with rays, about the size of her thumbnail, with a tiny diamond winking in the centre.

It looked like… Stella's mittened hand went up to touch her star pendant through layers of sweater and parka.

A whisper came to her ears. *Take it.*

She flinched back. *I can't!*

Take it! Hurry! Take it now!

The whisper was a fierce command. It gave her courage. She reached out.

A soft growl stopped her hand within an inch of the sun charm. The sound came from behind her. She turned around. Over by the ruined wall a dog, or something like a dog, stood watching her. Gaunt, wild, wolfish. It began to walk toward her, still growling softly. White teeth showed in its narrow jaws.

Stella took a step back, then another. Her heels teetered on the edge of a hole. She edged sideways, not daring to look away from the dog.

From the corner of her eye she could see the trail of black marks her boots had made in the frost. Those were the only marks. The dog had left no footprints.

That means it's not real. It can't hurt me. Can't even scare me.

At the thought, the dog's growl became a rumble. It was suddenly larger. Its head lifted to catch and hold her gaze. The pointed ears flattened. The slant-set eyes flashed silver-green. A feral look, yet almost human. A warning.

Stella's nerve broke. She turned and leaped for the nearest door, burst out and slammed it behind her. Then she leaned on the glass, gasping, hands clutching the handle.

Wait a minute: glass? Stella looked up and around. This was no ruin. No ghostly dance hall, either. This was the new, restored pavilion — again. A sticker right in front of her nose announced that the glass was tempered, reinforced, and shatterproof. That didn't make her feel much safer, though. She guessed it wouldn't stop the dog-thing.

Looking back in through the door, she saw no dog, and no golden sunburst twinkling in the centre of the space. The ice-crusted broken timbers were gone. Everything was as it was should be, clean and new and unfinished.

When Stella climbed down to the ice and set off again across the lake, she couldn't shrug off an itch of frustration. She'd walked all the way across the lake and nearly froze her face off, all to settle the questions in her own mind. And nothing at all had been settled. The questions had only multiplied.

That gold pendant: had it really been there? Maybe, if she'd tried to touch it, her hand would have gone right through it.

But somebody told me to take it. Somebody really wanted that. Who?

And the dog stopped me. Why?

There had been a battle, some sort of contest, with her in the middle. And somebody had lost. She had a strong hunch that she'd been on the losing side.

Chapter 11

STELLA WAS nearly halfway across the lake, so far as she could judge by the brightness of the lights on the south side, when a buzzing machine sound broke out behind her. She looked around. A light swept across her eyes, dazzling her.

It was a snowmobile, common enough in these parts, sometimes more common than cars. And it was coming straight at her. She waved her arms, hoping the driver was sober enough to see her before he ran her down.

The machine came to a sudden snow-showering stop within two feet of her. It sat throbbing gently. "What the hell d'you think you're doing?" said an angry voice from behind the glare of the headlight.

Stella squinted past the light. "Mike?"

"Looking to go for a polar swim, eh?"

"You mean... Oh, right." She felt stupid. This was something she'd known once, but had forgotten: that when a lake freezes, the ice forms from the shore outward. The centre is the last part to freeze. A good thing to remember on a dark winter night, if you wanted to go on living.

"You were heading straight for the thin ice! It's maybe a centimetre thick out there. A guy went through last week and he's just lucky his friends were around and knew what to do!"

"Okay, okay! I forgot." She crunched over to him and nudged his gloved hand. "Thanks for roaring out to rescue me. But isn't it even more dangerous for you to be out here? That sled must weight a ton."

"No, just about 500 pounds." Now that she was on the other side of the light and no longer blinded, she could see that he had his smile back. "But that's why I'm heading straight back to shore," he added. "And you're coming with me. Hop on!"

Stella didn't much like snowmobiles — noisy and polluting — but riding one, she had to admit, was something else again. The moonlit ice blurred past, the wind whipped her cheeks, the machine purred under her like a live thing.

And sitting behind Mike on the long seat, with both her arms wrapped around his waist, was ... well ... comforting. Almost enough to put dog-things with shining eyes out of her head.

They came to land a few miles east of the pavilion, then followed the shoulder of the Shore Road eastward. "So, what were you doing out here," she shouted over the hornet's whine of the engine, "this late at night?"

"Looking ... Edge," he shouted back. She caught only every second or third word. "Found ... truck ... gas ... left it..." He powered down the machine and brought it to a stop. "There's a place I want to show you," he said. "The Lookout. But you must know it."

"Yes, from years ago! Love to see it again."

He nodded and restarted the snowmobile. She clutched his waist before she could slide off backwards. They followed the Shore Road until it met a narrower road going north. Turned onto that, and Glimmer Lake dropped away behind. Fields of snow marked off by fences rose up, steeper and steeper, until fields were swallowed by forest. Ahead and above lay the long, icesheet-rounded hills, black against the stars.

They stopped, finally, at a place where a shelf jutted out from the face of a hill. A low stone wall ran around the outside edge. Mike shut off the snowmobile and silence rushed in. Almost silence. The only sounds were the sough of pine boughs, like distant surf, and the patter of blown snow crystals bouncing off the metal of the sled.

Glimmer Lake lay far below. It was glowing tonight. From this height it looked like an oval puddle of quicksilver. The lights of houses twinkled in the surrounding darkness. They were scattered and looked lonely, except where the town lay, a band of multicoloured brightness cupping the southern side of the lake.

"I wonder if I can pick out our house," Stella said. "It's second from the end on Bluejay Road. It has to be one of the last lights there on the west side of town." She searched with her eyes, but couldn't make up her mind if one of those lights was the one where Molly lay asleep on the sofa.

Thinking of that, she felt uneasy. Maybe she'd been wrong to leave Molly alone.

Mike leaned his elbows on the wall and just looked. He didn't seem inclined to talk. She prompted him. "You said you were looking for Edge and found his truck? What then?"

"I saw it had gas in it, so I left it there, next to that cabin — yes, I found the cabin, nobody there. I left the truck in case he comes back. He'll need wheels to get home."

If he's not lying frozen to death under a snowbank somewhere, she thought. Looking sideways at Mike's stony profile, she guessed he was thinking the same thing. She drew a breath and blew it out in a long icy plume. *Okay, let's get into it.* "Mike? When did you see the dog?"

He went still. Then tried a careless shrug. "What dog would that be?"

She held up a hand. "Don't say you didn't. Molly thinks you did, and she's good at reading people. She saw it at least once, she says. I've seen it twice. You?"

He shoved hands in pockets, hunched up his shoulders, and took several steps away, scuffing at the snow. She thought he wasn't going to answer. Then he walked back. "Okay, you're right. And I'm glad it's not just me. All the same, I wish I didn't have to admit it. I don't believe in stuff like that. Didn't used to, anyway."

"Me neither. Feet on solid ground, that's me."

He shot her a sideways grin and leaned on the wall again. "But there's not much to tell. It started after Edge began to change, a couple of months after Molly came to town. Times when he got shut away inside himself, when he didn't know I was there. Some of those times, I thought there was a shadow near him. I figured it wasn't a real shadow, it was just me, thinking dark thoughts."

He let out a short laugh. "And then one day I saw him on the street after work, and there was this animal at his heels. Plain as day. I asked him if he'd got a pet. We both looked down, and there was nothing there. We laughed about it.

"It happened a couple of times after that. Always when Edge was stuck in his thoughts, when he was walking somewhere, alone, not looking at anything. That shadow close behind him, sort of dog-shaped. It scared me worse every time I saw it. I wasn't sure if it was something bad that had latched on to him — because it *was* bad, I knew that — or if it was my own bad thoughts. I worried maybe I was going nuts."

She leaned beside him. "Well, you aren't going nuts, unless we all are. Why would this dog-thing start following Edge?"

"Don't know. Except.... Well, maybe there was something dark inside him that it liked." He gave her a fierce stare. "If anybody had a right to be messed up inside, it was Edge. You can't blame him."

"I don't!"

He pointed down and to the west. "See that track that breaks off from the hill road and pushes back into the upcountry, there? Right,

that one. Follow that road, and you come to a few little farms in between the hills. You know the kind. Or maybe you don't. Their best
crop is rocks. We grew up on one of those farms. Mom got fed up
and left when I was four and Edge was six."

"Oh, Mike!" She wanted to give him a hug, but something in his
face told her to keep her distance.

"Dad took ten years to drink himself to death." His voice stayed
flat. "So then we sold the farm, for not very much, and moved into
town. Edge has been working, supporting me while I go to school."

"Sounds like a hard life," Stella said softly. "And not only for
Edge."

"Mostly for him. He remembers our mother. I don't, not really. I
think he never got over her leaving. There's always been a shadow on
him."

"But this dog-shaped shadow…"

"Yeah. It's different."

"Did you see the green gleam in its eyes?"

"The what? I never even saw its eyes. It was never that clear, or
not for more than a second or two."

"Consider yourself lucky!"

"All right, Miss Macmillan. Over to you. " He turned to face her
again, hands in pockets. He was smiling now. A smile made a won-
derful difference to his face.

So she told him everything. He'd earned it. Pacing back and forth
to keep her feet from freezing, she told him about the dream she'd
had, and the dog in the hallway, the girl under the ice, and — taking a
deep breath, and bracing herself for his disbelief — the sight of the
old pavilion all lit up, and what she'd seen and heard there: sad ech-
oes of that long-ago dance.

And finally, the gold sunburst pendant hanging, unsupported, in a ruined hall. A whisper, *Take it!* And the doggish creature that defeated her.

She brought it all out in a rush. When she finished, and stopped pacing to face him, he nodded thoughtfully. "Six months ago I'd have said you were making it all up."

"Well, I'm not."

"I know. The thing that worries me… how come you can see this dog clearer than Molly or me?"

Stella knew what Molly would say ("You have Lily's gift!") but decided to let that lie. "None of this is helping us find Edge. What'll you do now?"

"Now? Go home. Get some sleep. Don't want to, but…" He rubbed gloved hands over his chin and cheeks, and Stella realized that a lot of that grim look of his was sheer stubbornness in the face of exhaustion. "I'd miss a lot by night, anyway. I'll start again tomorrow at first light." He walked toward the snowmobile.

"Isn't it time you went to the police again?"

"No!"

"All right, then, you'd better let me help search." She settled on the seat behind him.

"We'll see." He looked back at her over his shoulder. "Maybe I should just hang around Molly until Edge shows up at her door. He's bound to, sooner or later."

She couldn't tell if he was joking. Her question blew away with the snowmobile's roar.

Chapter 12

MOLLY WAS STILL sound asleep on the sofa, cuddled under her blanket, when Stella let herself into the house. She seemed warm and comfortable enough, and Stella didn't disturb her. Within ten minutes she was asleep herself, in the newly made bed in the spare room.

That night she dreamed again that someone was calling her. *Stella! Stella, wake up!* She woke with a feeling that someone had been standing by the bed, and had just gone. Not the dog, nothing hostile. Whoever had called her had left something in the air: a faint warmth, or a subtle fragrance that faded as she tried to identify it.

She sat up in bed and pushed her hair out of her eyes. *Why would I dream of being called? And who's calling?*

The room was in near-total darkness, but a little light fanned in the doorway, enough to show that the door stood half open. *I closed it last night. Oh, no... please, not...*

She slid out of bed and tiptoed to the doorway. Looking out into the hallway she saw nothing out of place. A long bar of moonlight stretched along the floor from the oval window in the balcony door, which was closed. No dog of any size, shape or colour stood there.

It occurred to her to wonder if Molly was still down on the sofa. *Better check on her.*

She left her doorway and headed toward the stairs. Two steps, and her foot came down on something that skidded out from under. She fell with a crash and a yelp of pain.

An answering shout came from downstairs. The hall light came on and Molly ran flapping up the stairs clutching a blanket around her shoulders. "Stella!" Molly knelt beside her. "Are you okay? How did you fall?" She looked around. "Why've you got these books out?"

"Books? What books?"

"Those books." Molly pointed. Five books lay in a row down the centre of the carpet runner, starting from the library doorway and ending near the head of the stairs. They all lay open.

"I ... didn't ... ow ... get them out." Stella sat up, rubbing her right hip. "I fell over them. You must have left them out."

"Me? Leave books on the floor? No way! That's one thing I'm careful about, my books." Molly pointed her chin at the open door of the library and crafts room. "They came from there."

Stella picked up the first and looked at the cover. "*Your Northern Garden*. Huh. And here's one on wildflowers."

"What's this ratty old thing?" Molly picked up a torn paperback. She flipped it over. "Christopher Marlowe, *The Complete Plays*." She stuffed some loose pages back in, slapped it shut and picked up a book with a bright cover. "This one's about Caribbean cooking, would you believe."

Stella picked up the tall, thick book at the end of the row, the one she had fallen over. "Look, here's a volume of our old *Encyclopedia of Animals and Birds*. Gosh, you still have that?"

"It's a weird mix. Even weirder, how did they get here?"

"You have poltergeists?" Stella was only half joking.

"Poltergeists that read? They could at least put their books away!" Molly closed the books, stacked them, carried them into the library, and set them on the floor beside the shelves. "I'll put them away tomorrow. Let's get back to sleep!"

WHEN STELLA stepped out of her room on Thursday morning, dressed in pyjamas, slippers, and fleecy red bathrobe, she took one look at the floor of the hallway and stopped dead.

"Molly!"

A groaning sound came from Molly's room.

"Molly, get out here! Right now!"

Bedsprings creaked and Molly shuffled out, rubbing her eyes. She was still wearing yesterday's clothes. Stella pointed at the floor. "Well?"

Molly stared. "Again!" She squinted at Stella. "Did you…."

"Of course I didn't!" A thought struck her. "Molly, have you started sleepwalking?"

"Don't be silly!"

"Then who…"

They stared at each other, then knelt down side by side in front of the row of books. The same five books, in the same order, laid out in a tidy row. Molly put out a hand to close the first one, then checked. "Wait…"

Stella sat back on her heels. "A message, you think?"

"Looks like it, doesn't it?" Molly elbowed her. "Though I'm surprised you'd admit it. You, all about evidence and logic."

"I just try to keep an open mind. And this is starting to look like evidence of something."

"No kidding. So we'd better leave them open until we know what's what."

"Priority number one: coffee." Stella stacked the five books on top of each other, still open, stood up holding the sliding stack in her arms, and started carefully down the stairs, step by step.

In the kitchen, while Molly boiled water to brew tea and coffee, Stella described last night's dream of being called. "Like somebody really wanted me to get up and find those books. But what for? And why me and not you? It's your house now."

"That's interesting." Molly looked up from pouring hot water. "Maybe you're the only one who can hear whoever-it-is."

Stella laid out the books on the kitchen table, with the encyclopedia on the bottom, in the same order they'd been found upstairs. "Right, what've we got? *Your Northern Garden. Ontario Wildflowers.* Those two are sort of related. *Hot Stuff: Caribbean Cookery.* Not related."

"Here's another odd man out." Molly tapped the open page of the *Complete Marlowe.* "Didn't we study one of his plays at school?"

"Yes, it was *Doctor Faustus.*" Stella glanced at where the book lay open. "And look what's showing there!"

"*The Tragical History of the Life and Death of Doctor Faustus,*" Molly read aloud. "Yeah, I remember. It was about a man who sold his soul to the devil." She shook her head. "Can't see what that tells us."

Stella leaned on her elbows and frowned down at the books. "Ha!" She sat back, smiling. "Got it! The first one: it was open at this section." She tapped the page.

"Cultivating bulb flowers," Molly read over her shoulder. "So?"

"This part's all about growing ... guess what? ... day lilies! And this one, *Ontario Wildflowers....*" Stella held it up to show a photo of a flower with spotted yellow petals. "Get it?"

Molly set down two steaming cups. She peered at the book. "Trout lily! Lily and Lily!" She did a little dance. Then dropped onto a chair. "And that means what, exactly?"

"Lily and Faust." Stella sipped coffee. "What do they have in common?"

"Nothing that I know of. Our great-grandmother did *not* sell her soul to the devil." Molly reached for the book on Caribbean cooking. "Maybe this will help."

"I've been back and forth over those two pages. They're useless. They're all about hot peppers."

"So let's leave it for now. I'm famished!" Molly went to the cupboard for cereal and a bowl.

Stella got eggs and bacon out of the fridge and turned on the stove. Over her shoulder she said: "Molly? Those herbal bundles of yours?"

"Well?"

"They're all up again, but something still got in. So obviously they aren't much use!"

"Wrong!" Molly wagged a finger in the air. "Those charms are made to protect against evil. Whoever or whatever left those books open is not evil. I know it in my bones."

They were halfway through breakfast (muesli with soy milk for Molly, bacon and fried egg on toast for Stella) when someone rapped on the kitchen door. A face peered in through the small window in the top half of the door. Stella leaped up. "It's Mike! Oh yikes, look at me!"

"Don't be silly, you're perfectly decent," Molly said comfortably, and crossed to the door.

"But my hair—" Stella clawed at it with her fingers. There was no time for anything better.

Mike brought in a billow of cold air and a shaft of milky sunshine. "Hi there. Nice morning." He nodded at them both, then grinned at Stella. "Late sleeper?"

"Not habitually," she snapped. "Coffee?" She went to get the carafe.

"Thanks!" Mike set his boots neatly in the rubber tray beside the door and straightened up, beaming. "Good news!"

Molly jumped from her chair. "You found Edge? Where is he?"

"No, I didn't find him, but I know he's alive. He's been around here — round your house — since last night. Maybe only hours ago. Check it out." He pointed at the window.

Molly and Stella crowded together at the kitchen window. A trail of man-sized tracks crossed the deep snow of the back yard, close to the house. "How do you know that was Edge?" Stella asked.

"I got a clear look at some of the prints. They're Edge's size, same as mine. Only, his right boot has a crack across the sole. You can see it in the print if you look close."

"That's brilliant, Sherlock." Stella handed him a cup of coffee. She looked out the window again and saw how the trail of prints had stopped under Molly's bedroom window. It looked as if Edge had spent a lot of time there, standing, maybe looking up, pacing back and forth. Her neck prickled. She hoped Molly hadn't seen that.

"I don't blame you for being scared," Mike said quietly. She looked up to find him watching her. "But at least it means Edge is alive and walking around. And it gives me a chance to track him." He gulped coffee. "Those tracks lead back over the lake."

"Suppose it snows?" Molly said. "Tracks won't last long then."

"I know. I'm out of here in two minutes." He glanced at the table. "What's with all the books?"

Stella explained, adding, "We can't see a clue in this one." She waved *Hot Stuff* in the air. "I'm thinking it got picked by mistake."

Mike took the book and ran his eye over the open pages. His eyebrows flicked up. "Huh!" He handed it back, grinning. "Scotch bonnets."

"Scotch bonnets?" Molly glared at the book. "That's a kind of super-hot pepper. So?"

"Well, bonnets — Bonnie. Right? I think her folks are Scotch, too." He walked over to the door and pulled on his boots. Then sent

Stella a quick smile. "Thanks for the coffee." With a rush of cold air he was out the door, closing it quietly behind him.

"Bonnets? Bonnie? Bonnie Orr?" Stella marked the place in the book with a sticky note.

"It's the best guess so far," Molly said. "He's a smart one, your Mike."

"He's not *my* Mike."

"Mm-hmm."

Stella flushed. "So: Lily, Bonnie, Doctor Faustus. What does that mean?"

"It must mean that we should go to Bonnie and find out what she knows about Lily." Molly scrubbed a hand through her mess of curls. "Look at me, I'm a disaster! Give me fifteen minutes to shower and change. You better get dressed too. Then we'll go."

Left alone in the kitchen, Stella remembered the last book in the row, the *Encyclopedia of Animals and Birds*. It belonged to a set of twenty hardcover volumes that her parents had bought second-hand to bolster their daughters' education. Molly hadn't been much interested, but Stella had read the books almost to pieces. The book on the table was volume *IG to LA*. It was frayed at the corners, the glossy photo on the cover dull with use.

It still lay open. Stella reached, looked, checked her hand. She fought the urge to step back, stepped forward instead and picked up the book. She stared. Closed the book on her forefinger.

Mike should know this.

Across the thought cut the roar of a snowmobile starting up. It snarled past the kitchen window and around the corner of the house toward the street.

"Mike!" Stella gasped. She flew at the kitchen door, thought better of it and raced to the front of the house. Wrestled open the front door, scurried out, slithered down the front steps. "Mike! Wait!"

He was already out on Bluejay Road, past the house. "Mike!" she screamed, but no amount of screaming was going to reach him past the snowmobile's roar. She dropped the book, scooped up a double handful of snow, briefly shaped it and hurled it hard and straight. The snowball shattered on the back of his helmet. He yelped, braked and brought the sled skidding around to a halt close to the sidewalk.

"What was that for?" he yelled.

"Need to show you something!" She picked up the book and held it up.

He got off the snowmobile and crunched back over the compacted snow and up the walk to where Stella was waiting. "Must be important," he said. "Aren't you cold?"

She remembered then that she was still in pyjamas, bathrobe and thin woolly slippers. Until that moment she had not noticed the cold. Now she began to shake. "L-let's make it fast. This b-book was one of the five we found last night. See that?" She tapped the page.

He took the book and stared down at it. She added, "You said th-that one time you saw the sort-of-dog thing with Edge, p-plain as day. W-was it anything like that?"

He nodded slowly. Then looked at Stella with eyes that had gone dark in a colourless face. They looked together at the picture that took up half of a page. The long, thin legs, the gaunt tawny-furred body, bushy tail, ears long and pointed like a fox's, muzzle sharp and narrow, yellow eyes set slantwise in the flat head. Wild, dangerous, hungry-looking.

"That's what I saw too," Stella said, careful and calm. "Only, not."

"Um, yeah. This thing," he touched the photo, "would run if it met a human, I bet."

"The thing I saw wouldn't. Didn't."

"But why," he cleared his throat. "Why a jackal? A golden jackal?"

"Why not a golden jackal?"

"We don't have any kind of jackals around here."

"Mike, do you really think what we saw was a real, live, natural animal?"

"That doesn't answer my question, but no. And more than ever I need to find Edge." He closed the book and handed it back and nudged her toward the house. "Go in. Get warm."

Stella could no longer feel her toes. As she tottered back along the walk and slithered up the steps, she thought: *I better show this to Molly.* Then: *No. Not yet.*

She hadn't told Molly about her trek across the lake last night, or what she'd seen in the pavilion. She didn't want to share this news about the jackal, either.

Keeping information from Molly made her feel guilty, but she told herself she needed to think about it first. There was too much she had to settle in her own mind before facing Molly, who for sure would gloat about powers and gifts and other things Stella had always scoffed at.

Chapter 13

"YOUR GREAT-GRANDMOTHER?" Bonnie set two bowls of steaming bean soup on the counter and added side plates of buttered whole-wheat toast. "Why ask me?"

Stella had anticipated this question and had been thinking how they should answer it. There was no way to tell the truth without adding to Molly's reputation for flakiness. On the other hand, she wasn't going to lie. "We'd like to know more about her. And, well, your family's one of the oldest ones in Glimmer, right? We thought you might've heard something, anecdotes passed down... You know."

Bonnie made a thinking-about-it face, then shook her head. "Not really. But your own family must be full of Lily stories, right?"

"Lots of stories, no real information," Molly put in.

"Well, you could always ask — oops, hold on, ladies." Bonnie strode across the room to greet a large and hungry-looking farm family who were organizing a long table for themselves and needed extra chairs. Stella and Molly were well into their soup before Bonnie came trotting back, only to vanish into the kitchen.

They got the rest of it after Bonnie had served the farm family. "You could ask my gran," she said.

The original Bonnie Orr had kept house for Lily for twenty-five years, until Lily grew so frail she had to move into a nursing home. After that, Bonnie went to work in her husband's diner, taking charge completely when he died. She retired only three years ago.

Stella cleaned her bowl and licked the spoon. It really was good soup. "Would she talk to us about Lily, d'you think?"

"No harm in asking. I'll phone and find out."

The answer was yes. "She wants you there at four this afternoon, for tea," Bonnie said. It sounded like a summons. And it probably was, Stella thought, remembering the woman she'd nicknamed Mrs. Ogre.

The day seemed endless. Stella got Mike's phone number from Molly and called him twice, hoping to find out how his search for Edge was going. He never answered. The second time she left a message, telling him their plans for the late afternoon.

Molly opened Magic by the Lake sharp at nine a.m. and did a brisk business. In between waiting on customers, she made up another dozen St. John's wort bundles. "Heavy-duty industrial strength version," she said. "I've added verbena, for protection against evil influences, and actual horseshoe nails."

"You're planning to sell these?" Stella asked hopefully.

"No, they're for us. Three over each bedroom window. Don't roll your eyes."

Stella tacked them up as directed. After that she shovelled the latest fall of snow off the front walk and the sidewalk in front of the house. Then surfed the internet looking for references to golden jackals.

There wasn't a lot that was helpful, aside from the physical description. The golden jackal, also known as the Asiatic jackal or reed wolf, was a canid native to north and northeastern Africa, southeastern and central Europe, Asia Minor, the Balkans, the Middle East, and Southeast Asia. It was omnivorous, adaptable and mostly nocturnal, tolerated arid conditions well, and was a swift and tireless runner.

In some Indian and Nepali folk tales, jackals were portrayed as malevolent and treacherous. That at least seemed to fit. On the other hand, real-life golden jackals were intelligent and monogamous (they mated for life), trained the older pups to help take care of the younger ones, and appeared to be all-round solid citizens.

MRS. BONNIE ORR lived in a little white house at the end of a pine-darkened lane north of Glimmer Lake. The hills hulked like sleeping bears behind it. Molly and Stella had cut miles off their trip by skating across the end of the lake. Coming to land, they put on their boots, carried their skates by the laces, and walked the rest of the way.

It was exactly four o'clock, and the sun was behind the hills, when Molly knocked on a polished wooden door. Stella was glad Molly was in front when the door swung open, because she couldn't help staring.

Bonnie Orr looked much the way Stella remembered. The same high-piled, dead-black hair, the same large and impossibly white teeth, the same ferocious horn-rimmed glasses.

But now she saw that the hair and teeth were plainly fake. The thing that startled her most was that Mrs. Orr was tiny. The icy-sharp grey eyes were barely level with her shoulder.

Not an ogre, she thought. A gnome!

"Well? Come in!" Mrs. Orr snapped. "I'm not paying good money to heat all outdoors."

"A blessing on this house," Molly said, with a graceful wave, as she stepped inside. She handed Bonnie a sprig of greenery.

Bonnie held it up between thumb and forefinger. "What's this?"

"It's fennel and oak for good health and long life, and marjoram, for peace."

"Huh!" With pencilled eyebrows arched high, Bonnie set the charm gingerly on a table. "I've been hearing things about you,

Molly Macmillan." She set hands on hips and looked Molly over, toes to crown of head. "Wiccan, eh? What's all that baloney?"

"With respect, Mrs. Orr, it's not baloney. As you must know."

"And how would I know that?" The grey eyes narrowed.

"Obvious. It runs in our family, and you knew Great-Grand-mother Lily well." Molly smiled gently, gravely. "You must be aware that she was Wiccan at heart."

Bonnie showed her big white teeth. "Never! She was a strong Presbyterian. If she were alive she'd give you an earful, miss!"

"Ah, I don't agree. If you consider—ow!" She broke off and gave a Stella a wounded look.

Mrs. Orr grinned. "Well, come along, get your coats off. Tea's ready. Good thing you're prompt."

As they followed her along the narrow hallway to the kitchen, Molly breathed on Stella's neck: "Why'd you kick me?"

"Lay off the white witch stuff," Stella murmured back. "It won't work here."

The kitchen was small, but scrubbed and shining. Bonnie sat them down at the pine table laden with plates of hot buttered cinna-mon toast, a big pot of strong black tea, milk in a peach-coloured glass jug that looked as old as Bonnie herself, and sugar in a match-ing bowl. The mugs were thick white china that looked as if they came from the restaurant.

"That really hits the spot!" Stella said a few minutes later, hold-ing out her mug for a refill.

Mrs. Orr flashed a grin with those enormous teeth. "Heard about you, too. You look like Lily."

"I didn't know that." Stella pictured her great-grandmother as she'd last seen her, a wrinkled wisp that looked as if a breeze would blow her away. "Can you tell us what she was like, when she was my age?"

"Ah! At last!" Without another word, Bonnie pushed her chair back and left the room. Stella and Molly looked at each other.

"What?" Molly whispered.

"No idea," Stella whispered back.

A few minutes later Bonnie came back carrying a large, flat cardboard box. After opening it and folding back layers of tissue paper, she lifted out a big, old-fashioned photo album. The cover looked like padded leather. Stella and Molly jumped up to clear the table and make a clean space for the album.

Bonnie set it down, then placed a hand flat on the cover. She looked sternly from Molly's face to Stella's. "I knew you would come along, sooner or later. 'Keep this safe,' she said to me, 'until somebody comes and asks for it.' I'm guessing she meant the two of you."

"She?" Stella asked.

"Lily."

Molly looked puzzled. "But if she wanted us to have it, why didn't she just mail it to us?"

"Maybe you had to show you were ready," Bonnie said. "Maybe you had to ask."

Stella and Molly exchanged a baffled look.

"Well, take a look!" Bonnie opened the front cover. Someone had written *The Craigs of Glimmer Lake* on the first thick black page in beautifully formed flowing silver letters.

The next turn of the page opened on a photograph that took up half the leaf. It was held in place by little silver paper corners. Two girls sat side-by-side on the white steps of a verandah, with their hands clasped over their knees. It was summer, judging by their short-sleeved dresses.

"That's Lily, age nineteen." Bonnie's gnarled finger hovered over the taller girl on the right. "You see?"

"Wow, you're right," Molly said.

Stella nodded, but she hardly glanced at the girl who had been Lily. She couldn't take her eyes off the other girl: smaller, fairer, and a couple of years younger. The face that smiled out at the camera was radiantly beautiful.

What really kept her gazing, unable to look away, was this: the girl was the same one she had seen under the ice yesterday.

Chapter 14

"BONNIE, THAT'S amazing!" Molly said. "Lily does look like Stella, quite a lot. Same eyes, same mouth. Same expression — like she's saying, 'Just try and put one over on me!'" She laughed.

"You do too," Bonnie said, "only not so much. You haven't her strength."

"Huh," Molly said, not looking pleased.

Stella cleared her throat. "Who, uh, who's that?" She pointed at the other girl in the photo. "Is that…"

"Aurora," Bonnie said. "She would've been sixteen when that was taken. Summer, 1925."

Molly whistled. "What a stunner! Why couldn't I've inherited those looks? Oh, wait, that's the one who died."

"That's right. They had big plans for Aurora, so Lily told me. She was expected to marry well. Year and a half later she was dead and gone."

Stella studied the older girl's face. A strong face, even at nineteen. *Does that really look like me? No way!* "Was Lily with Aurora, that night when the pavilion collapsed?"

"Yes, she was there too. Lily was twenty then. Nearly two hundred were killed. She was one of the few who survived."

"We were both just babies when Great-Gran died," Molly put in. "We never got to know her. You lived with her twenty-five years. You must have come to know her really well. What was she like?"

Again Bonnie studied Molly's face, then Stella's, as if debating whether they deserved to be told anything at all about their great-grandmother. Finally she pursed her mouth and nodded. "So. What was she like? She was a good woman. Honest. Smart. And kind, as kind as they come. But not a softie, oh no!" The big white teeth flashed. "Nobody ever crossed Lily Macmillan: or never more than once."

"Whoah! Bit of a dragon, eh?" Molly said.

"She could be." Bonnie touched Lily's pictured face with a gentle fingertip. "I always thought there was grief at the back of that. I think she was grieving all her life."

"Grieving?" Stella echoed. "For Aurora?"

"Most likely. She hardly ever talked about that time. But it's my belief she never got over what happened at the pavilion. I believe she blamed herself. Though Lord knows what she could have done to stop it."

"Did she ever...." Molly dipped a hand into the collar of her shirt and pulled out her moon pendant on its thin gold chain. "...ever say anything about these? Show yours, Stel."

Stella pulled out her star pendant and held it out beside Molly's. "They were Lily's," she explained. "She left them to me when she died."

Bonnie leaned over to peer at them. "No, she never mentioned anything like those. Pretty things. But hold on, now. Where have I seen something like that before?" She screwed up her face to think and shook her head. "No... It'll come to me. Have some more tea."

They were halfway through a second pot of tea, and leafing slowly through the album, when Bonnie said, "Ah!" She went out of the room and came back with a thin leather folder. "Lily kept this at the bottom of her old steamer trunk. I'm guessing she never liked this fellow much."

She opened the folder to show a large studio photograph of Aurora with a young man. The pose was typical of the era. Aurora sat straight-backed and graceful in a richly upholstered armchair, hands folded in her lap, feet demurely crossed at the ankles. Her pale dress had the sheen of satin. A double strand of pearls circled her throat.

The man, slim and dark, stood behind her and a little to her left. His right hand rested on her left shoulder in a gesture that Stella thought looked possessive, his fingertips pressing down.

"Who's this guy?" Molly held up the folder to read the inscription. "'Aurora Craig, Heath Frost. Engaged December 1926.'"

"She doesn't look all that happy, does she?" Stella said. Heath wore a small, fixed smile, but Aurora's beautiful face could have been carved from marble.

"Reason I thought of it?" Bonnie tapped the image. "Look at her wrist."

Stella and Molly bent their heads together over the folder, blocking out the light. "I can't see a thing!" Molly complained.

Stella tipped her head and narrowed her eyes to see. "Bonnie, have you got… oh, thanks." A reader's magnifying glass slipped into her hand. She focused it on Aurora's wrist, and stared. Then handed the magnifier to Molly.

Molly squinted, then lifted her head. "I don't believe it! There's a third!"

"Yes, and she had them all right there, look!"

Aurora was wearing a charm bracelet on her left wrist. It bore three charms: a crescent moon, a five-pointed star, and a sun with rays. Stella thought of the girl under the ice holding up her left wrist, with something shining on it. She thought of last night's vision of a sun-shaped charm spinning in a ruined hall.

Heart beating fast, she touched her own charm. The moment she did, everything changed.

ICE, FRESH SNOW, dazzling sunshine — a perfect winter's day. Aurora's hair streamed like spun gold in the breeze as she skated. Her red scarf, no redder than her cheeks, snapped like a banner. She laughed when Lily's woolly hat flew off and Lily went chasing after it, scolding.

Out of nowhere came Heath Frost, quiet and knifelike as his skate blades. "A word, Miss Aurora?" he said in that lovely lion's-purr voice of his. "Look, here's a trinket I found on my travels. It made me think of you — although its beauty falls far short of your own. Won't you accept it?"

He took from his pocket a small white leather box and opened it. Inside, bedded on blue silk, lay a gold bracelet, its charms brilliant in the sun. Very pretty and elegant; and also, she guessed, very expensive.

"It's lovely! But you know I can't." It would be unseemly for her to accept such a gift from Heath, or indeed from any man unless she planned to marry him. He knew that perfectly well.

"Then only try it on, so I may see how it looks on your wrist. You may take it straight off again and give it back." His voice grew darker, softer. "Please? Then I will have that memory, at least, to take away with me."

She hesitated. Then, because it would have been rude, even cruel, to refuse him such a little thing, she said: "Just for a moment, then."

Smiling, he fastened the bracelet around her left wrist.

The instant the gold touched her skin, the world receded: the ice, the sun, the whistling wind. Silence came down around her like a cage made of glass. In the silence she heard him whisper: "This is what you are to me, Aurora. You are my sun, moon and stars. My whole world. Forever."

His arm was around her then, as if it had a perfect right to be. She wanted to protest, but the words would not come. His eyes gazed into hers: dark, hungry, eating her up.

Lily came skating up, out of breath. Heath smiled. "Hello, Miss Craig. Caught your hat, I see."

STELLA BLINKED. The dazzle of sun and the slap of icy wind were gone. She was someplace warm, dark, and smelling of cinnamon toast.

She looked down at the photograph on the table and trembled. Heath's pictured face was alive. The small smile was meant for her. Something looked out at her from the dark eyes. A green gleam winked and was gone.

She gasped and stepped back. When she looked again the photo was just a photo, lifeless and still.

Chapter 15

"WELL, THAT was an eye-opener," Molly said, as they walked down the lane from Bonnie's house. It was already dark, so close to the solstice, but the bright moon reflected off the snow and showed their way between the ranks of pines.

Molly was carrying both pairs of skates, one pair slung over each shoulder. Stella carried the photo album and leather folder in a canvas shopping bag, along with a tin of Bonnie's homemade shortbread.

"If you mean about Bonnie, absolutely," Stella said. "I'm ashamed to think I ever called her Mrs. Ogre."

"She still doesn't approve of me, though, with my wicked Wiccan ways." Molly laughed. "But I really meant it was useful, what we learned. Whatever's been going on, the charms — the three gold pendants — are at the heart of it, and it's been going on a long time. I wish we had that letter of Lily's, the one that came with the pendants. Remember? You were twelve at the time."

"All I can remember is how Travis looked when he read it. He was hopping mad!"

"Hopping? Travis?"

"Yeah, you know, in that controlled way of his. And he said something about 'dangerous garbage,' and 'not the sort of thing that a young girl should be exposed to.' I think he wanted to tear it up, but the letter was for me, and you know what Travis is like."

"Honest and good and not an ounce of humour." Molly sighed.

"He told me I could have it when I was eighteen. Hey, that means I should've got it on my last birthday!"

"He must have forgot. Let's get straight home and phone him. Who knows, it might explain everything! Which reminds me, I need to get a new phone. I think my old one's lost forever."

Molly fell silent then. Stella was rather glad. She needed some peace and quiet (on Molly's part) to sort out in her head all the things that had happened the last couple of days.

"And there's a lot to explain," she said. "I know, I know, I've been in denial. And there are things I haven't told you, just because I didn't understand them myself. I still don't. I'll talk it out, if you'll listen. And Molly, try not to interrupt, if you can stand it, okay?"

A murmur came from Molly's side of the path.

"Okay. You see, I've seen a lot of strange stuff. One or two things I could shrug off, but it's starting to add up. Last night, after you fell asleep..." She told what she'd seen in the pavilion, including the gold sunburst charm and the doggish creature. "And there was that voice, like a whisper in my head. Someone wanted me to take the charm. But how I could take something out of a vision, I don't know. Although it did seem very real."

"Mm," Molly said. Their two pairs of boots squeaked in the dry snow, the only sound in this still night except for Stella's voice.

"Then last night and today, that weird business of the books. The message. Lily, Lily, Faust, Bonnie. And the last book, the *Encyclopedia of Animals and Birds*. Guess where that opened? A piece about the golden jackal." She summed up what she'd learned of that animal. "Not that that helps us much. Why a jackal? That's what Mike said. He's right, it doesn't make much sense, even in the skewed, nutty logic of superstition, does it? There's a black dog in the story of Faust, remember? The black dog was a hellhound, or a familiar, or some kind of demon. But this thing I saw looked like a golden jackal. Only not. It looked... *more*."

"And then just now at Mrs. Orr's, I had a vision. Or something. It was so real, it's like I was there. When I looked at that photo, suddenly I was Aurora. Out on the lake with Lily, skating. I know Heath did something to me, I mean Aurora, when he put the charm bracelet on her arm. It was like a, a cage for her mind."

Molly murmured and her shadowed head nodded.

"Then, when I came out of that, I saw something in that engagement photo that made me think of the jackal. Its eyes..." Stella shuddered. "Heath had that same green gleam in his eye, the same look of ... it's hard to put in words. Wild, intelligent. Animal, but human as well. Ferocious. Terrifying."

Stella realized she'd been waving her free arm. She laughed. "Thanks for being such a good listener! Yeah, I know, you think I've got a closed mind. Well, I am sceptical about most of that paranormal stuff: not like you, big sister. I have to balance you off, right?"

Molly murmured something.

Stella shifted the heavy bag to her other hand. "But when I saw that gleam in Heath's eyes, in the photo, things changed for me. That was not imagination, it wasn't a dream, it wasn't a trick of the light. That was real. And it's like a door opened and I stepped through and on the other side there was... I don't know. Someplace strange." She looked up at the shimmering stars and drew in a deep breath of frosty air. "Now I'm back through the door, but I know the strange place still exists somewhere, and it's real. Just as real as this snow we're walking on. And, Molly—"

She stopped and turned to catch Molly by the arm. Molly wasn't there. Stella looked up and down the lane. There was nobody else in sight.

How long had she had been walking alone, talking to a shadow? A shadow that seemed to answer.

"Molly!" She dropped the canvas bag in the snow and ran back up the lane toward Bonnie's house. No sign of Molly, but there were the skates, sticking out of a drift by the side of the path. She left them there and pelted back down the lane, heavy-footed in her boots, in and out of black tree-shadows and white stripes of moonlight.

Stumbling out on the Shore Road, Stella looked along it both ways and saw nobody and nothing. Then movement caught her eye. Not on the road but beyond it, past the guard rail and the icy-crusted boulders of the shore, out on the frozen lake. Someone was out there, far out, close to the centre. In the moonlight she saw them clearly. Two dark figures struggling.

She scrambled over the guard rail, stumbled over the boulders, fell, struggled up, ran on. Far ahead the two figures lurched back and forth. Near them lay a smear of something dark and shiny. A patch of open water.

She was still many strides away, far beyond reach, when the smaller figure broke free and teetered on the edge of the broken ice.

"Molly!" Stella strained to run faster. She hit a patch of bare ice. Her feet flew out from under her. When she scrambled up there was only one black shape huddled on the ice. The smaller one was gone.

SHE'D BEEN half aware of an engine's whine swiftly growing louder at her back. It swooped down on her now as she slithered onward, screaming "Molly! Molly!"

"Get on!" Mike shouted. She threw herself at the seat, the sled leaped forward, and moments later it skidded to a halt.

Stella pitched off and scrambled up again, already running. The patch of black water was two strides away, and it was empty. No. Something there. Fingers broke the surface.

"Molly!"

Next moment she sprawled full-length. Mike had tackled her and brought her down. She fought to get free. "It's Molly — we've got to—"

"Not that way! You'll just drown along with her!"

"But—"

"We do it like this! You stay back!"

Flat on his stomach, Mike crawled forward. Stella hardly breathed, watching, crouched on hands and knees. The huddled black shape on the other side of the break didn't stir. She paid it no attention.

Water splashed. Molly's face rose, gasping. "Hold on!" Stella shouted.

Mike was almost within reach of Molly's flailing hand when the ice beneath him made a snapping sound. Stella cried out. Mike lay dead still. Then inched forward and the ice cracked again.

"No!" Stella yelled. "You're too heavy! Get back!"

"No time!" He started to crawl forward again. Water oozed from cracks on both sides of him.

"Back!" Stella took hold of Mike's ankles and yanked with all her strength. She pulled until she had him well away from the cracked section. She never took her eyes from the patch of black water where Molly's face bobbed, almost submerged.

Mike hadn't fought her. He sat up, white-faced. "Stella—"

"I'm lighter!" She was already down flat and crawling over the ice, well away from where the cracks showed. Beneath her the ice creaked and gave slightly.

Nearer, nearer. Mike shouted encouragement. She saved her breath. Nearly there!

And then she was there, the broken edge of ice under her chin, Molly's face inches away. Molly's eyes stared, unfocused. Her hand groped weakly. Stella reached and grabbed it.

At the same moment a face rose beside Molly's. Bone-white, bone-thin. Eyes: black holes with a gleam of green fire deep inside. *She's mine,* a voice whispered in Stella's mind.

"No!" Left hand cinched around Molly's wrist, she lashed out with her right at the bone-white face. Her fist passed through a stun of cold.

The bones grinned. *You can't watch her forever.* The thing sank and was gone.

Chapter 16

"GOT HER?" came Mike's shout.

"Yes!"

"Hold tight!" Hands grabbed Stella's ankles and dragged her backward, away from the broken edge. She gripped Molly's right arm tighter, then caught her flailing left and felt joyful that Molly was still able to move.

A long minute later they clung together on solid ice. Molly's hair and parka were leaden with water and beginning to freeze. She was barely conscious, eyelids drooping, hands and face icy and as white as ... Stella thought of the other face in the water, and shoved the thought aside.

With Mike's help she peeled off Molly's parka and flung it aside. Then pulled off her own and tugged it on around Molly, pushing her flopping arms into the sleeves. She dropped her mitts to zip up the parka, then pulled the mitts on over Molly's stiff hands, and her toque over Molly's drenched head. The wind bit into Stella's unprotected head and body. She started to shake.

"Mike! We've got to get Molly home, *now*, before she freezes!"

He was bending over the other huddled figure. "Edge?" The figure stirred.

"Mike!"

He looked up. "I can't leave him. You'll have to take Molly back yourself. On the sled."

"But I don't—" She stopped. Looked down at Molly, slumped against her side, under her arm. "Show me how."

Mike helped her half-lift, half-push Molly onto the snowmobile. Stella climbed on in front. Mike took off his jacket and made her put it on, cutting her protest short. "If you're too cold you'll never manage the controls." He pulled a bungee cord out of a saddlebag and wound it several times around their two waists. "That should hold her up long enough. You'll need both hands to drive. Take my gloves."

"But you — okay. How do you make it go?"

"Easy." He turned the ignition switch. Over the engine's roar he shouted: "See those things on the handles? They're the brake and the throttle. Brake's on the left. Grip the throttle with your right to speed up, ease up on it to slow down. Steer with the handlebars." He scooped up Molly's saturated jacket and stuffed it into the saddlebag. "Now go!"

And it was easy. Or it would have been, if Stella hadn't already been clumsy with cold, despite Mike's heavy jacket and gloves. Reaching the south shore, she was just able to find and enter the trail that climbed the bank and then ran along the shore eastward. Where it came out onto Bluejay Road she almost hit the fence post that marked the trail's end. She swerved and nearly hit a tree. Then she overshot their house and had to turn the sled, slowly and awkwardly. She stopped in front of their house so abruptly that Molly toppled off into a snow bank, dragging Stella with her.

It took almost the last of Stella's strength to unfasten the bungee cord and lever Molly to her feet. "I can walk," Molly muttered, and fell over again. She began to crawl on hands and knees. Stella levered her up again and together they struggled as far as the front door. Molly leaned against the door while Stella pawed at the handle. It didn't budge. She remembered it was locked, staggered back to the sled, pulled Molly's parka from the saddlebag, and found the key in a zippered pocket. Unlocked the door, pushed it wide. They fell inside together.

"You need to be in bed." Stella thought of the stairs, around behind the dividing wall, through the PRIVATE door. No way they'd manage that trip, short though it was. But there was still a blanket on the sofa in the shop. She brought that, and with shaking hands spread it out on the lobby floor.

Molly was pawing vaguely at the parka zipper. Stella pulled it off, then worked off the wet sweater and pants underneath. Rolled her onto the blanket and covered her up. Staggered upstairs for more blankets. Molly soon looked like a woolly cocoon curled up in the coat alcove.

Stella thought of Mike struggling to get Edge moving, thought of Mike tramping coatless across the ice. "Molly, I'll be back! Soon! I promise!" Molly murmured and burrowed into the blankets.

Stella flung off Mike's parka and pulled on her own, cold and damp from contact with Molly's soaked body. Catching up Mike's coat and gloves, she ran out into the night. She met them twenty paces out from shore, holding each other up as they lurched along, bare heads bent against the wind. She climbed off the snowmobile and bundled Mike into his own coat, then bullied the two of them onto the sled. "Molly's house!" She slapped Mike on the shoulder. "Go!" He went.

WHEN STELLA got back to the house, the lobby was deserted. "Molly?" she shouted in sudden panic. "Molly!"

"Hey there!" Mike called from the kitchen, and came to meet her in the hallway. He carried a mug of what looked like hot chocolate. "Thanks for rescuing us," he said, smiling. "Edge wouldn't have lasted—"

"But where's Molly?"

"She's okay! Edge carried her upstairs. I'm just taking this up."

"Edge? You let him get at her?" She flung off her mitts and leaped at the stairs.

Mike followed more slowly, careful with the steaming cup. "Stella, it's all right!"

"You crazy? He tried to kill her!"

"Stella—"

She burst into Molly's room and skidded to a stop. A figure that looked like Mike's ragged shadow knelt at the side of the bed, his arms on the blanket, his eyes on Molly's half-hidden face. "Keep away from her!" Stella darted forward.

Edge glanced at her, then fastened his gaze on Molly again.

"It's all right," Mike said from the doorway. "He's himself."

"Oh really? How can you be sure?"

"I know him. I'm sure." He walked around her to the bed and held out the mug of hot chocolate.

Edge slipped an arm under Molly's head, took the mug and held it so she could drink. Stella never took her eyes from him. When Molly had taken a few sips she turned her face away and nestled against the pillow, her eyes drooping.

Stella looked at Mike and tipped her head at Edge. "Out. Both of you."

Mike turned toward the door. "Okay, we'll go home. Edge, come on."

"No!" Molly whispered. "Stay here. Safe."

"Well, okay. Out of the room, though." Stella stepped close to Mike. "Thanks for everything," she said quietly. "I owe you. It's just..." She glanced at Edge.

"I know." He tapped his brother on the shoulder.

Edge got up off his knees, placed the mug on the bedside table and followed Mike out, looking back at Molly at every second step.

Stella sat on the edge of the bed and touched Molly's nose, which was almost all that could be seen above the blankets. "Safe? It's not his safety I'm worried about."

"I... trust him."

"Molly, have some sense. First he kidnapped you. And now he tried to drown you!"

"He didn't..." Molly's eyes were closed, her voice a thread. "I thought I was talking to you... then it was Edge. We were out on the ice and ... I fought and... he fell down. And then the shadow was there. I backed away... fell in. It was Heath ... tried ... drown me."

"Heath." Stella thought of the bone-white face in the water. She shuddered. "But Edge took you out on the ice. He's working for Heath, or Heath's controlling him, somehow. I suppose you think your sprigs of green stuff will keep the evil whatsits away from him while he's in this house?"

Molly didn't answer. She was asleep.

Chapter 17

WHEN STELLA left the bedroom, closing the door behind her, she nearly fell over Edge. He was sitting in the hall just outside Molly's door, still in his ragged, dirt-stained denim jacket, hugging his knees. Mike sat beside him.

Edge lifted his head. "Is she going to be all right?"

It was the first time she'd heard him speak, or seen his face up close. He sounded completely normal, which surprised her. He looked a lot like Mike, only thinner and older, and his hair was matted into black spikes. The brown eyes were the same, though. She thought of how gentle he had been with Molly just now.

"I hope so."

She sat down on the hall carpet cross-legged, facing the brothers. "All right, let's have it." She nudged Edge on the knee. "Explain to me just what the hell you were trying to do to my sister out there!"

"Not to hurt her! I swear! At least, I didn't mean..." Edge sank his face onto his knees, then looked up. "I can't recall much of the last few days. All I really know is that I had to stay close to Molly. Me and... the other one."

"What other one?" she said sharply.

"Go easy on him," Mike said. "He's had a rough time too."

"It's okay, kid. She has a right. The other..." He looked at her again. "For a while, months, maybe, I knew there was somebody close to me. I could never see him. He was always just behind me. Sometimes he was in here." He touched his chest. "I felt what he felt. A horrible..." Edge shook all over. "...longing. Like a sick man in a dark room. Hungry for sunlight. Sunlight..." His eyes grew vague.

Stella tensed, ready to move fast if she had to. Mike watched his brother's face.

"And he paid so much to win her," Edge murmured. "Such a terrible price he paid... how can he give her up?"

"Give who up?" Mike asked. "Molly?"

"Molly? No! Aurora."

"Aurora!" Stella echoed.

Edge looked at her with empty eyes. "Lily, take care. He hates you so much!" Then he blinked, shook his head, and stared around in confusion.

Lily. He called me Lily. Stella's hand clasped her star pendant through her sweater. With the other hand she touched Edge on the wrist. "Is he still in there with you?"

"No, he's gone. He won't come back. I won't let him."

She held his eyes: warm brown now, no confusion and no shadow. He thought what he said was true, and maybe it was, here and now. But for how long?

Edge yawned enormously, closed his eyes and all at once began to slide sideways down the wall. Stella helped Mike hoist him up and guide him into the spare bedroom. "The two of you can share it tonight. Let me get my things out."

She moved her belongings to Molly's room. Better I stay close to Molly tonight anyway, she thought, as she slid in beside Molly's gently snoring form. Make sure she's safe.

But as sleep enveloped her she wondered: had they let the enemy into the house?

STELLA WOKE, shuddering with dread. A dream had just faded: the now-familiar dream of being called, and warned, by some benign presence. As it faded, her sense that something horrible was coming grew strong. Whatever it was, it was near, and getting nearer.

She opened her eyes and pushed the covers down from around her face. The night was not as dark as she'd thought at first. Moonlight made a glowing rectangle of the window and pasted a shining lozenge on the floor.

Wait a minute, Stella thought groggily. That's not right. The curtains were closed. I closed them. Shouldn't be this bright.

The glow was bright enough to show that the other half of the double bed, the side farthest from the window, was empty. Stella tensed, then relaxed. Molly's just gone to the bathroom, she thought. She turned over.

Something white drifted near the window.

She froze. Only her eyes moved. The white thing turned and Stella went boneless with relief.

"Molly! You nearly scared me to death!"

Molly was ghostly white from neck to heels in her silk-knit long underwear, which she was still wearing from last night. She didn't answer, didn't seem to have heard.

"Molly?"

The one eye Stella could see was wide and shiny, reflecting the glow from the window. What was this, sleepwalking? Molly had never sleepwalked in her life! But that's what this looked like. Maybe she'd opened the curtains in her sleep.

Stella sat up. What to do? It was dangerous to wake a sleep-walker, or so she'd heard. But suppose Molly opened the window — because it looked as if she was about to do just that — and fell out and hurt herself?

She looked past Molly to the window. Something moved at the edge of the frame. A cluster of pointy shapes touched the glass. As they slid away from the frame, she saw that the pointy things were joined at the base. It was a hand. Stella's heart crowded up into her throat.

A hand on the end of a long, thin, white arm was sliding across the window like a snail.

It was getting hard to breathe. Stella's head swam. She dragged in a lungful of air. *It can't get in. The window's locked. It can't get in.*

A step away from the window, Molly slowly lifted an arm. Her fingers found the thumb-latch at the top of the lower sash. She began to turn it.

In half a second Stella was across the room. She yanked Molly's hand away, took her by the shoulders and steered her back to bed. Molly stopped with her knees against the mattress and stood staring, blank-eyed. Stella gave her a push and she fell forward.

Quick! Grab the blanket and flip it over her, tuck it under her on the other side. Roll her over so the free end of the blanket was underneath. Wrapped like that, Molly wouldn't be able to free herself without waking up.

Stella spun around and faced the window, hoping to see it empty. But the white arm still stretched across. The hand splayed flat on the glass behind the latch.

It can't get in. The latch is on this side. It can't...

Untouched, the latch began to turn.

Chapter 18

STELLA FLUNG herself again from bed to window. Grabbed the latch and twisted it shut. Inches from her eyes, the bone-thin hand on the other side sucked at the glass like a leech. The latch began to turn again. She forced it closed. It pushed back. She held it, both hands straining, while it struggled against her aching fingers like something alive.

It wasn't staying closed. She was losing the fight. The latch turned, turned...

The bedroom door slammed open. Another hand knocked hers aside and grabbed the latch. A shriek of rage pierced Stella's head. She clapped her hands to her ears.

Mike let out a chestful of air. "Wow! Hey, it's okay. I think it's gone."

There was no hand on the glass now. Stella pressed her face to the window and looked down. The snowy yard was empty. She jerked the curtains shut.

"Oh... my..." Her legs felt ready to melt like warm wax. But there was no way she was going to collapse in front of Mike, who looked amazingly calm. She straightened up. "Did I yell?"

He shook his head. "Edge woke me up. He said there was danger."

"Help!" A muffled voice came from the direction of the bed.

"Oops — Molly!" Stella went over and helped Molly unroll from her cocoon, while Mike turned on the light. Molly sat up and shook back a wild mop of curls. "What happened?"

"You walked in your sleep."

"No way! I never sleepwalk! It was more than that, wasn't it?" Her hands went to her mouth. "The dream. Oh, holy.... That was Heath at the window! What happened to my protections?"

Mike pointed. "You mean those things?" Tiny, prickly green bundles littered the floor below the window. "You must've taken them down in your sleep... or trance, or whatever it was."

"You know what this means?" Molly's voice shook. "Heath doesn't need Edge any more to get at me. He can get at me himself, directly." She buried her face in her arms.

Mike and Stella picked up the protective charms and fastened them around the window again. By the time they'd finished, Molly was back to sleep. "That hypothermia really wiped her out," Stella said.

"You need your sleep too," Mike said. "We all do. Wait a sec." He went out and came back a minute later, with a blanket over his arm. He faced Stella and stood at attention. "Permission to bed down in front of the window, ma'am." He was all but saluting. It looked like a joke, but it wasn't.

She looked from him to the window, eyebrows raised. Then at Molly, innocently asleep. She nodded slowly. "The floor will be hard. And cold."

"I've slept rough before. Oh, and Edge will be lying down outside the door." He tilted his head in that direction.

"I... well... Thanks, Mike." She suddenly wanted to kiss him. *Uh-uh. Keep things cool.*

It was just past four a.m. by the clock radio when she turned out the light and climbed into bed for the second time that night. She didn't expect to sleep much. She was right.

"COUNCIL OF WAR," Molly said over the breakfast table on Friday morning. She was still pale and inclined to wobble, but insisted she couldn't sleep any longer. "Besides, I don't want to be by myself. I need to be with you guys."

"Council of war?" Mike dug a fork into his scrambled eggs and bacon. "Right. If we're going to win, first we need to get things straight. Work out what we know and what we don't. Stella, you start."

"Me? Okay. The first night I was here, I had this dream. At least, I thought it was a dream. Maybe it wasn't." In between bites of egg and toast, she told them again about the warm presence that woke her, then faded, and the gaunt doglike creature in the moonlight.

"Then there were the lights in the pavilion. I saw them Tuesday and Wednesday, before the actual lights were wired in. And then the girl I saw under the ice, that was Aurora. And then…" She described what she'd seen at the pavilion on Wednesday night. "And yesterday I had … I guess it was some kind of vision … in Bonnie's kitchen. I saw Heath giving Aurora the charm bracelet. He did something to her then, I'm sure of it."

"He's still around, too," Molly said. "Still trying to get into people's minds, trying to possess people."

Edge ducked his head and pushed away his dish of buttered toast, which he had been devouring in hungry bites.

"Go on, eat! You're skin and bones." Mike pushed the dish back at him. "Okay. We know Heath, or this jackal thing, or maybe they're working together, is after Molly's moon pendant, and he was trying to use Edge to get it. But he's failed. Maybe he'll give up now and leave us alone."

"Not a hope!" Molly shook her head fiercely. "He wants my pendant and he wants it bad. That has to mean he wants Stella's too, because they belong together. They were once part of that bracelet he put on Aurora. But *why* does he want them so badly?"

"And why," Edge said quietly, "are Heath and Aurora still haunting the lake after so many years?"

"That's easy, at least in theory." Molly looked smug. "Unfinished business. There are things they have to do. That's the main reason ghosts stay stuck in this world."

Stella poked her on the arm. "You know that for a fact, eh?"

"We-ell, nobody really knows, but that's the, um, consensus." Molly looked less smug and raised her mug of peppermint tea for a gulp.

"So answer this one. Why has he been attacking you and not me? We both wear pendants."

"Obvious. I arrived here first. And also, I'm easier meat." She poked the mug at Stella. "You're the one with Lily's powers. He may even be afraid of you."

"Afraid? Of me?" Stella laughed. "Didn't look like that, the first night, when the critter was actually in the house, a metre or so away, sizing me up."

"I've got more questions," Mike said. "Like, we know *who* Heath was, he's the guy who was engaged to Aurora all those years ago. But *what* was he? What is the jackal and what's it got to do with Heath? And if that bracelet is so important to him, how did two parts get separated and one part get lost? And where is the sun charm?"

"And," Stella said, "who or what put out those books that led us to Bonnie?"

Molly clutched her head. "Yi! My brain is spinning!"

"Mine, too." Stella rubbed her tired eyes. "I wonder where the pavilion fits into the puzzle? Too bad Great-Gran Lily's not still alive to fill in the gaps."

"Brilliant!" Molly dropped her hands and beamed at Stella. "Lily's letter! We need it now! Quick, go phone Travis and get him to find it. Tell him to scan it and send it as an email attachment."

Glad to have something simple and practical to do, Stella went into the store and dialled Travis's phone number in Nanaimo.

"Stella!" he muttered into the phone. "Wha ... what's wrong?"

She thought of telling him everything that was wrong, then decided against it. "I need Lily's letter."

"You need what?" He sounded dazed.

"Great-Gran Lily's letter," she explained patiently. "The one that came with the pendants, when I was twelve. The one you wouldn't let me read. Remember?"

A long silence on the other end. Then a groan. "That!"

"Yes, and would you please—"

"You woke me up at five a.m. to ask me about a crazy old letter?"

"Five?" She glanced at the time display. "No, it's eight ... oh, right. Sorry."

"It's the dead of *night!*" He sounded wide awake now, and furious.

"Oh, Trav, it's not exactly ... Okay! Okay, I'm sorry! But we need that letter. Can you please find it and—"

"No! Call later when I'm awake!" The receiver crashed down. Stella winced.

When she came back to the kitchen, Edge and Mike were washing and drying the dishes. Molly had covered the table with an assortment of herbs and bits of yarn, wood, and shell, and was deftly making up a new charm. She looked like a fisherman tying a fly.

"This is for Edge." Molly looked up, beaming. "He'll have the protection of the Goddess wherever he goes. I'll make one for you too, Mike."

"That's real nice of you." Mike smiled as he wiped a mug. "But, no thanks. I can protect myself."

"So can I," Stella said.

Molly sighed and shook her head.

Chapter 19

EVERYONE had plans. But before anyone had a chance to go any-where else, Stella persuaded Mike to start up the snowmobile and give her a lift around the lake and up the lane leading to Bonnie's house. The skates and the canvas shopping bag holding the precious photo album still lay where they'd fallen in the snow the night before. Nothing was damaged, nothing was even wet.

After bringing Stella home again, Mike collected Edge and they set off to get the pickup truck, still parked by the cabin in the hills. "After that," Mike said, "I'm driving Edge to the medical clinic in Barry's Bay for a checkup. He looks totally wrecked. He's going to see a doctor if I have to tie him up and haul him there."

Molly insisted on opening Magic by the Lake at nine o'clock. "It's business as usual," she said firmly. "I'm not going to spend the day cowering in bed, biting my nails!"

Stella impatiently waited until ten a.m. — seven a.m. Pacific Time — to phone Travis. He was halfway through breakfast, and had geared down from furious to merely grumpy. "Lily's letter, eh? All right, I'll look for it. If I can find the time."

"*Please* find the time, okay? Trav, this is important!"

"Why?"

Stella decided to tell the truth. She owed him that much. After all, he was their brother. "Because we're being haunted, and the pendants are the key to it all, and we think Lily's letter might explain some things."

"Haunted." Travis made a liquid noise: coffee going down, Stella guessed. "Okay, leave it at that. I'm sorry to see Molly has sucked you into one of her silly games."

"It's not a game, Travis!"

"Right. Well, the letter's still in the house, probably among the older documents. If I can find it, and I don't guarantee that I will, I'll send it along."

After hanging up, Stella went into the dining room/office to send Travis an email from Molly's computer, to make sure he had the address.

About one o'clock, Mike phoned from Barry's Bay. Stella took the call. "How's Edge?"

"Getting antsy. We haven't seen the doctor yet, and it might take another couple of hours. There's a full waiting room. Seems like half the people here have the flu."

"That's a pain." But a tone in Mike's voice caught her attention. "Something's wrong, isn't it?"

"Maybe. Maybe not."

"What's wrong?" Molly asked from across the store, where she was refilling a display of incense sticks. Stella waved a hand: *Give us a sec.*

"There's just this," Mike said. "A few minutes ago I saw a dog, or a sort of dog, in the waiting room, sitting under a chair behind this old guy's legs. Hard to see under there, but I'm certain he was watching us. The dog, I mean."

"You mean the jackal."

Molly dropped a box of incense sticks.

"You're sure?" Stella went on. "Suppose it was just an ordinary dog?"

"In the clinic waiting room? Dogs aren't allowed. Besides, next time I looked, the old man was still there, but the animal wasn't.

Stella, this Heath guy hasn't given up. That's why I called. Be careful. Okay?"

"Yes." Stella's heart sank into her stomach. "You be careful too." She hung up and told Molly what Mike had said.

"So he hasn't quit. All right," Molly said, as they crawled over the floor together, picking up incense sticks. "Here's what we'll do. We'll destroy the pendants."

"Destroy them? But can we? Should we?"

"Why not?" Molly stood up and started sorting the sticks by scent and colour.

"Well..." Stella couldn't come up with a reason why not. "It makes sense, I guess. It's the obvious thing to do." Still, the thought of harming her star pendant made her uneasy.

"Of course it makes sense! Then Heath will stop haunting us. And Aurora will be at rest. They'll have nothing to stick around for, you see? No more unfinished business."

Stella nodded slowly. "But how would we do it?"

"That should be simple." Molly flashed a confident smile. "They're gold, and gold melts easily, right? We can probably melt them in the oven."

"All right, we'll give it a try. But not until Mike and Edge get back."

"What's the matter?" Molly gave her arm a poke. "It's the answer, I'm sure of it!"

"Sure." But Stella wasn't sure, and for almost the first time in her life she couldn't explain why. She hated feeling this way: adrift in a cloud of uncertainty.

"NO," EDGE SAID. "Wouldn't work. You'd need a lot more heat than your oven can give."

The boys had come back at the end of the afternoon, just as dusk was closing in. Edge was basically healthy, the doctor said, but run down. He needed rest and proper food. ("Exactly what I could have told you," Molly said. "You didn't need to waste the day in a clinic waiting room for that!")

"What would do it?" Stella asked. "A potter's kiln?"

"It would," Edge said slowly. "But where..."

"There's at least three potters working within thirty kilometres of here," Molly said. "I know because I buy their stuff."

"So," Stella began.

"Not one of them would let us use her or his kiln without a lot of questions we wouldn't be able to answer."

"Okay," Mike said. "Welding torch. Right?"

"Right." Edge nodded. "An oxyacetylene torch would do the job, no problem. I could borrow one from Mr. Lennox. At least, I could if he hasn't washed his hands of me."

"Let's go and find out," Mike said calmly.

It was past eight when the pickup again pulled up beside the house. Mike climbed out carrying something that looked to Stella like a miniature suitcase. Edge climbed out after him, then lifted a rack holding two steel cylinders from the back of the truck.

Molly met them at the front door. "Not in the house." She waved toward the back yard. "We'll do this on the shore, out from under the trees. You never know how magical objects might react on being destroyed. The effects might be quite violent."

"That's reassuring," Mike muttered.

Molly led the way along the lane and past the house, walking straight and solemn, like a priestess leading a procession: impressive even in the Hudson Bay blanket coat she was wearing while her parka hung to dry in the basement. The coat's stripes of bright colour turned black and grey in the moonlight, giving Molly the look of a shaman wrapped in an animal's brindled skin.

And she was fully conscious, Stella knew, just how impressive she looked. Edge was certainly aware of it: he couldn't take his eyes off her.

Bringing up the rear, Mike nudged Stella and whispered, "You sure she's not... you know..."

"Putting mojo on him?" Stella laughed under her breath. "Just the normal kind."

"Here." Molly stopped at a large, flat rock on the shore, a few steps up from the ice. Under the brilliant moon, everything gleamed. Quartz crystals glittered in the rock. When she slipped her moon pendant from its chain and set it down on the rock, it made a tiny pool of light.

"Now yours, Stella-Star."

"All right." Stella unfastened the chain at her neck and slowly slid the star pendant into her hand. Every move she made seemed to be pushing against something that pushed back.

Edge and Mike had the torch assembled and connected to the gas cylinders. "Ready," Edge said. He had pulled on heavy gloves and a pair of welder's goggles to protect his eyes. "Before this starts, all you guys stand back. There could be flying bits."

With a sound like rushing wind, a plume of blue-white flame sprang from the nozzle of the torch. Edge stood aside, waiting for Stella to set her star on the rock beside the crescent moon.

"Come on, Stel!" Molly danced from foot to foot, no longer dignified. "My toes are freezing!"

"All right! Here goes."

One last time, Stella closed her hand tightly on the tiny star. Its points dug into her palm. Weird to be so attached to a little bit of gold! She leaned forward to set it down.

SHE FLOATED, arms out like wings, not sure if she was flying or swimming. She wondered briefly where she was. Suspended in air, or water? Everything in this place was blue and cool. Above her head it lightened a little, but not much. Beneath her feet it darkened.

The drowned girl, the one under the ice, floated beside her. Those luminous sapphire eyes were smiling, yet they looked sad. Her hair eddied around her face like liquid gold. The silky dress, not peach-coloured now but green as sea-glass, swirled against her body.

"You must tell her." Aurora held up her wrist, to show the chain bracelet bearing one charm: the one shaped like the sun. "Tell her."

Stella shook her head, scattering bubbles. "Tell who?"

"Lily, of course. Tell her."

"Tell her what?"

"That it was not well done."

"But what did she do wrong?"

"She should have taken all three. She should have freed me."

Strangely, that hurt, sharp as a knife in the gut. "She tried!"

"Not hard enough. She damaged his spell, but not completely. She didn't break it." Aurora drifted sideways, fluid as seaweed. Her eyes were huge and reproachful.

"Aurora — she — we — I'm sorry—"

"Your regret is useless to me. So long as I wear *this* I suffer a half-death. Always fearing him, always fleeing him. Never finding rest."

"Then give it to me!"

Aurora's eyes lit up eagerly. Then she slowly shook her head. "I can't."

"Why not? Give it to me and we'll destroy the charms, all three!"

"I can't, not here." Aurora glanced over her shoulder. Beyond and below her, the blue depths seemed darker than before. She dipped her head close to Stella's and whispered. "Meet me at the party."

"You mean...."

"Yes, at the pavilion. The grand Christmas party. I'll give it to you then, if I can. But until then, there is something you need to know. Fire..." She broke off and swirled around, peering through the growing gloom. Something was moving in the depths.

"What's wrong?" Stella stared. "What's out there?"

"No time. Listen! Fire will not destroy the triple charm. All you can do is—" She gasped. "He's coming!"

In a whirl of green and gold, she was gone. A whisper came back. *Get away! Hurry!*

Stella floated, her heart pounding. She could guess who or what was coming. Get away, right! But get away how?

I don't even know where I am, or how I got here. Where can I run?

A shape was forming in the indigo shadows, something pale. Cold currents washed over her body. She floated backward, shaking with more than cold. The shape grew larger, more solid. Skin, bones. Human, but less than human. It swam at her, shark-like, opening its jaws. Green fire burned in the places where its eyes should have been.

Chapter 20

"STEL?" SOMEONE was shaking her arm. "Wake up!"

"Stella? Are you all right?" Mike's voice.

She focused on his face. He was holding her by the arms and peering anxiously into her eyes. Molly leaned in from one side.

"Yeah, I..." She freed herself to rub at her eyes, and found the star pendant still clasped in her fist.

"Looks like you went away for about thirty seconds," Molly said.

"I... I did. I was... dunno. Someplace else."

"Like that time at Bonnie's?"

"Y-yes." Her hands were shaking. No wonder, they were bare. She dropped the pendant into her coat pocket and pulled on her mittens.

Edge still held the torch, but the flame was off. He'd pushed the goggles to the top of his head. Stella nodded at him. "Might as well pack that up. It won't do any good."

"Who says?"

"Aurora."

"Oh."

They stood in a circle around the stone, looking down at Molly's moon pendant through clouds of breath vapour. "Well," Mike said at last. "Ghost or no ghost, I can't believe gold won't melt at — what is it, three thousand degrees Celsius?"

"A bit more," Edge said. "Worth a try." He looked a question at Molly, who shrugged, then nodded. Then he looked at Stella. She hesitated, then fished the star charm out of her pocket and set it on the rock beside Molly's.

"All right, everybody back." Edge settled the goggles over his eyes. The blue-white plume of flame hissed from the torch. He played it over the pendants. They didn't change, except to gleam brighter, as if they were being polished.

Mike frowned over Edge's shoulder. "Should be liquid by now."

Back and forth the flame moved, and still the tiny gold star and moon sat there unchanged. Suddenly the rock split with a gunshot crack. The two charms leaped into the air and bounced back down. Molly swooped in to catch them, but Edge stuck out an arm to stop her. "Don't touch the rock! Hot!"

Mike unfolded a pocket knife and carefully flipped the charms off into the snow. Molly scooped them up gingerly in her mittened hands and held the two of them close to her eyes. Then tipped them over and studied the other side of each. "No change. None at all." She smiled at Stella, pulled off a mitt and picked up the star. "Aurora was right. Here, take it. No, it's not hot. It's actually cold!"

"Just like me. Let's get inside!"

"SO WE'RE GOING to the party after all," Molly said thoughtfully, fifteen minutes later. The torch and its gear had been stowed in the truck, and now three of the four were nursing mugs of hot chocolate in the shop's book nook. Mike had built a fire in the fireplace, using kindling and split logs from a box beside the hearth. Edge lay in the recliner, wrapped in blankets, eyes closed.

Stella had reported what useful (as far as she could judge) information had come from her vision. She'd avoided any mention of what she'd felt: the terror of the shark-like bony shape, the sadness of Aurora's reproach. And the strange feeling she'd had then, and still had, that she and Lily were being reproached together, as if they were partners in blame.

"Well, I'm going," she said. "Nobody else has to."

Mike frowned at her from the armchair across the room. "What makes you think you can wrap this thing up all by yourself?"

"And where," Molly said sternly, "do you think you'll get a ticket? I'll call Joyce tomorrow morning and tell her I've changed my mind. You," she waved her mug at Stella, "can come along and help decorate the pavilion. Earn your pass."

"Me? I suck at decorating!"

"You can be the gofer. Tote ladders, hammer nails."

"Oh, fun!"

"What about me and Edge?" Mike demanded.

"The tickets will each be for a couple," Molly said sweetly. "And we'll need dancing partners."

"Good," Edge said sleepily, still with eyes closed. "I'm no dancer, though."

"I'll coach you." Molly smiled at him, then winked at Stella. "Star can teach Mike."

Stella didn't mean to catch Mike's eye, but she couldn't stop herself. She felt her cheeks heating. Mike grinned. "I don't need teaching. I'm already pretty good."

"And conceited! Well, if you're so good, you can teach me," Stella muttered crossly. She frowned a "no matchmaking" message at Molly, who winked back.

And then, with one of her quick changes of mood, Molly set down her mug, rose to her feet and fixed Stella with a somber look.

"I think it's time I gave in."

"Huh?" Mike said. Edge opened his eyes. Stella just waited.

Molly unfastened the gold chain from around her neck and slid off the moon pendant. She held it out. "Take it, Stella-Star."

Stella looked at it, then at Molly. "Why?"

"Because you have the strength to protect them both. I can't even protect this one. It's safest with you."

It was on the tip of Stella's tongue to refuse. But then she thought of Molly locked in a shack in the hills with a half-crazy Edge... Molly struggling in icy water with something long dead ... Molly entranced, reaching to open the window to the enemy.

Suppose Molly lost the pendant, next time? Worse: suppose Molly didn't survive the next attack?

Would I do any better? Stella wondered. *I haven't been tested. Looks like it's my turn now.*

She looked up again at Molly and nodded. Molly said, "All right, then."

Stella stood up and Molly, in a strangely formal manner, reached up and unclasped the chain from Stella's neck. Then she slipped her moon charm onto Stella's chain, so that it slid down and tinked against the star. She refastened the clasp at the back of Stella's neck and stood back.

"There." Molly suddenly looked worried. "I hope this is the right thing to do."

Stella looked up and was surprised to see Mike and Edge both standing, silently watching, as if they were attending a ceremony. As if she'd been awarded a medal, perhaps. She looked down at the two charms gleaming together on the front of her sweater. She'd almost expected to feel something: a prickle of electricity, or a burst of warmth. But there was nothing.

Not quite nothing. The two charms together felt heavy. She'd never noticed the weight of the star alone, it was so small. Something in their weight sparked a memory.

"Aurora said something just before she scrammed. Something

about the charm. What was it?" She held the charms together tight in her fist. As if they were a key turning in a lock, the memory opened. "'Fire will not destroy the triple charm.' That's what she said."

"Triple," Edge repeated, and Molly's eyes widened.

Mike looked baffled. "Well, we know there's three."

"She meant more than that." Stella looked from face to face. "She said 'the triple charm,' not 'the three charms.' There's something about these three pendants that's special when they're together."

"They make a unit," Molly said. "They want to be one. That should mean they'll grow stronger as they're combined. Maybe even when just two are combined."

Stella tucked the chain and pendants inside her collar. She felt safer when they were hidden away next to her skin.

"Two together," Mike said slowly. He looked worried.

"I wonder," Molly said, "if Heath had them, would the two be strong enough to bind Aurora again?" She sat back down. "Is that why he's so desperate to get the two we have?"

"Well, he can't get them if we stick together. He can't hurt any of us, either. Safety in numbers, right?" Mike glanced at Stella, then turned away.

"Molly?" Edge asked quietly. "We stay here tonight, Mike and me?"

"Sure. Best plan." Molly was brisk, but her cheeks were pink. "It really is best," she added, after the boys had gone into the kitchen to make sandwiches.

Stella raised eyebrows. "So why the blushes?"

"Well, I mean, how long can we keep this up? Edge and Mike here, I mean."

"So the neighbours are buzzing? Since when did you ever care about what people say?"

"I don't! I care about what Edge says and thinks. I just want him to be safe. And happy. And, and proud of me."

"That's a lot to just want." Stella slipped an arm around Molly and gave her a hug. "But it's only until tomorrow, I hope. Aurora was trying to tell me how to set her free. There'll be another chance at the party."

"A ghost at the dance?" Molly laughed. "That will be so cool!"

"Weird, you mean."

"As if there's anything about this business that *isn't* weird!"

Molly trudged upstairs, yawning. Stella went into the dining room/office to wake up the computer and check on incoming email, then followed her up. "Nothing from Travis yet," she announced, as she came into the back bedroom and closed the door. "Could he have lost it?"

"Trav, lose a legal document? Because that's what the letter is, you know." Molly stopped, half in and half out of pyjamas. "He wouldn't, not in a million years. He can't have looked yet."

"I vote we phone him right now. Shake him up."

Molly shook her head. "Bad idea. That would just put his back up. Then we'd have to wait weeks to get the letter." She crossed the room to look out at the lake. "No glimmer tonight," she said. Then, "Oh! Look!"

Stella joined her at the window. Across the lake, a tracery of golden lights shone on the far shore. You could make out the shape of the dome. "So they have the wiring done. Pretty!"

"Is that like what you saw, those other times?"

"No, nothing like. This is, well, electric lights. That was ..." *Time slip, memory, dream.*

"I know," Molly said. "Magic."

"WHAT WAS IT like?" Molly murmured into the darkness.

Stella was drifting, half asleep. "Wha...?"

"The place where you met Aurora. What was it like?"

"Mm." Awake again, she thought about it. "Hard to describe."

"Try."

"She ... Aurora ... said she was 'suffering a half-death.' I think, where she is now ... it's like the place where she died. In the cold, in the dark, in the lake..." She shivered. "Only, bigger. Endless. I think she's stuck there forever unless we set her free."

"I've never felt anything like that," Molly said softly, muffled in blankets. "And I guess I never will."

"You wish?" Stella turned over and stared at the back of her sister's head. "Don't tell me you're envious!"

"Only a little bit. Mostly, I'm grateful." She sighed. "I used to wish I had real powers. But after what we've been through, I'm glad I don't!"

Chapter 21

STELLA EXPECTED a bad night with disturbing dreams, fading presences, and voices calling her name. *Who was it that was calling me, those other times?* she wondered as she drifted off for the second time. But no voices woke her. And if there were dreams, she didn't remember them.

Saturday morning, the day of the Festival of Lights, she woke to a late, red dawn. Molly was already up and at the window, pulling the curtains aside. "Look! Isn't that glorious?"

Their window faced north and a little east, but the sunrise advertised itself over the whole sky. Scarlet light dyed the white curtains and bled onto Molly's face and hands. Stella sat up and stared uneasily, but Molly was smiling when she turned around.

"Glorious." Stella stretched and rubbed her eyes. "You know what they say about red sky at morning."

"Sailors take warning." Molly laughed. "No problem. No sailors here!"

AFTER BREAKFAST Mike and Edge went home to their cramped rented house on the south edge of town. "You two will be over at the pavilion, helping out," Edge said. "You won't need us. Lots of people around."

"Right," Mike put in. "You'll be fine, just don't go wandering off on your own."

He was looking at Stella as he said this. She felt warmed and annoyed at the same time. "Hey, I'm not three years old!"

The boys went into the lobby to pull on their coats. Standing in the shop, Stella overheard her own name. It was Edge speaking.

"Sure, you're worried about Stella," he said. "It's your girl who has the charms now. But, kid, that means you're in danger too."

Stella backed off, heat rising in her cheeks. She was glad to hear the front door open and close.

Your girl. Well, maybe that was what Edge thought. She wasn't so sure it was what Mike thought.

As she started upstairs, another phrase crept forward from the back of her mind. *You're in danger too.* She sat down on a step to think about it. Why would Edge say Mike was in danger now?

It didn't take long to work it out. Edge had not been in any danger until Molly brought the moon pendant to Glimmer. Only then did he begin to change. Heath had shadowed him, invaded him, because he was the one person who was really close to Molly: close to the pendant.

But now Stella had the pendants, both of them. And yesterday Mike saw the jackal. "Watching us," he'd said. But suppose it was watching only him? Waiting its chance to get into him. To get close to Stella.

Sitting in the dark stairwell, she set elbows on knees, dropped her face into her hands and thought of Mike. How much she liked him. How she dreaded what might happen to him if she dragged him into this kind of danger.

I should send him away. Just tell him thanks, that's it, goodbye. But would it do any good? Would it keep him away if something got at him? And would he be safer close to me?

I might just be shooting both of us in the foot.

She raised her head. Invisible eyes were watching her: she could feel them. For one moment the dark corner at the bottom of the stairs

seemed to hold a darker shadow than what should be there, something animal-shaped and crouching.

She looked again and nothing was there. *Of course there's nothing there!*

She stood up and started up the stairs again, stubbornly not
glancing back at the base of the stairs. No need to worry about Mike,
she told herself. Mike wasn't like Edge, everybody said so. Mike was
rock-solid, both feet on the ground.

He'd said it himself: there was a sadness in Edge, a touch of
shadow that had opened a door for Heath.

But Mike was different. There was no darkness in him.

MID-MORNING, Molly and Stella skated across the end of the lake
to the pavilion. The red dawn had faded into a grey day, with a few
snowflakes whirling down an arctic wind. The forecast was for storm,
but just how bad a storm was still anybody's guess.

When they reached the pavilion it was already lit up, a bright arc
against the dim hills. Cars and pickups and snowmobiles were pulling
into the parking lot. Other skaters were sitting on the deck unlacing
their skates. Joyce waved at Molly and Stella through a window.

For the next five hours Stella forgot about ghosts, undead lovers,
or anything but the here and now. She was too busy holding ladders,
draping twisted ribbons up pillars, and tacking sprays of holly and
cedar on the arches over the windows.

The sky darkened and the wind blew harder as the hours passed.
Joyce worried that if the weather grew much worse, people would
stay away from the party.

"They won't, not this party. Not unless it really dumps on us,"
said Bonnie Orr. She had arrived at noon, clip-on reindeer antlers
crowning her sunset-pink hair, to supervise the unloading and organ-

izing of food supplies. Stella helped her carry boxes and set up tables near the bar.

About three-thirty in the afternoon, she finished tacking up one more gold-sprayed sprig of holly, reached down for the next, and realized there were no more.

"We're done!" Joyce called. "Woo-hoo! Great job, everybody!"

Stella and Molly gathered with the other volunteers in the centre of the pavilion and looked around. The six-sided hall, all sparkling glass and wood freshly painted white, had been transformed into a magical winter forest. Silver branches and sprays of greenery sprouted from every post. Swaths of spangled gauze hung from the ceiling with tiny golden lights caught in their folds, creating a mistily glowing sky. More spangles dusted the floor. The bar was crusted with blue and silver tinsel, and looked like the entrance to a treasure cave.

"Way cool!" Molly said. "Fabulous! And look how the windows reflect it all." The glass under the arches all around redoubled the points of light. Outside, daylight was already growing thick and blue.

This was the shortest day of the year, Stella remembered. Standing at one of the windows, looking out past the reflected lights into the snow-flecked twilight, she shivered suddenly. *No wonder we light all the lights, this time of year.*

There was always that ancient fear of the dark. Fear that this time the sun might not come back. That the dark might win. And the things that lived in the dark.

She touched the pendants through her sweater and thought of Heath for the first time since arriving here in the morning. She wondered what he had been before he became a thing of darkness. He must have been ordinary and human once. What had changed him?

Something touched the other side of the glass near her face. A

---

shadowy face with gleaming eyes. She gasped and stepped back, but it was only Mike, smiling at her through the mirrored lights. He waved and walked around to the front door. She headed across the floor to meet him.

Molly got to the door first. "How's Edge?"

"Still not a hundred percent. He may not be able to come to the party." Mike looked unenthusiastically around at the hall. "So you're done."

"Not come?" Molly's face fell. Then she frowned at Mike. "You don't mean he still thinks he might … you know … attract evil influences?"

"No, he just feels really tired," he said flatly. "I came in the truck. I can give you girls a lift home."

"That's great," Stella said, "but we're not done. We have to clear away all the tools and boxes and whatnot."

"You can help." Molly took him firmly by the arm.

The work was completely finished by four o'clock. "Thanks, everybody!" Joyce waved a handful of envelopes. "Free tickets! Come and get 'em!"

It wasn't until Stella climbed into the cab of the pickup beside Mike, and Molly handed in their skates and squeezed in after her, that she realized she faced disaster.

"Clothes!" she yelped.

Mike said nothing, just put the truck in gear and started off into the wind-blown snow.

"What about clothes?" Molly asked. "Oh, you mean party clothes?"

"Yes! I have nothing to wear! I only packed jeans and sweaters and all like that. We've been so busy, I forgot about dressing up."

"And you can't borrow my things, sad to say. They wouldn't fit."

"Not to mention our styles are completely different."

"Never mind, this is a blessing in disguise." Molly cheered up. "An urgent reason to shop for clothes! Mike, don't take us home. Drop us off on Queen Street, okay?"

"Sure." Mike drove in silence until they reached the corner of Queen and Market streets, across from the OPP station. Stella climbed out of the cab after Molly, then held the door and looked back at him. He was studying the traffic, his face turned away.

"Thanks for the lift. Will you pick us up for the party?"

"If you like," he said distantly.

"Only if you want to go yourself, of course."

"I'll be there, even if Edge won't."

"Then I'll find out if you really can dance," Stella said, keeping things light.

He reached over and pulled the door shut, then wheeled off, his tires showering snow.

Molly and Stella stood in the snow-laced orange glow of the streetlight, looking after him. Stella felt an odd little gnawing pain under her breastbone. "Well. Okay," she said flatly.

"Okay what? Boys have moods too, eh?"

"Moods? You know for a couple of days I thought he liked me. Talk about a brief encounter!"

"Of course he likes you!" Molly grabbed her hand. "He's worried about Edge, that's all."

"Then he's more worried than he wants to admit." She wondered suddenly if it had been Mike's idea to keep Edge away from the dance, because maybe he didn't trust him. But she didn't want to say so to Molly.

"Come on!" Molly tugged her along the street toward a store that was even more extravagantly decorated than the others. "This place has some amazing stuff. Amazing for Glimmer, that is. I come here all the time."

The Rainbow Unicorn did sound and look exactly like Molly's kind of store. Even so, Stella managed to find an outfit she could wear without feeling like a character who'd strayed into the wrong movie. A dress like a waterfall, all silky blues and greens, with a daringly plunging neckline and long, narrow sleeves that nearly covered her hands.

"There's a hint of wistful medieval maiden about it," she said, as she turned back and forth in front of the mirror. "But I can live with that for one night."

"You'll knock 'em dead!" Molly danced in a circle around her. "I don't know if I can stand you looking so gorgeous."

THEY PICKED UP take-out chicken on the way home and were in the door by six. Stella kicked off her boots, dropped the skates and her Rainbow Unicorn bag on the floor beside her coat, and skimmed through the shop and into the office where Molly's computer sat on the old dining table.

She had checked Molly's email that morning before they left for the pavilion. Nothing from Travis then. This time... Stella moused down the list of incoming emails, then called through the doorway to the kitchen, where Molly was opening the chicken boxes. "Still nothing! I'm phoning him!"

"Call him at work, it'll be mid-afternoon for him."

"But this is Saturday! Oh, right." Travis never really took a day off. She went into the shop, picked up the land line and punched in his number.

He picked up on the second ring. "Stella? Why... Oh, good grief! Well, it should be there. I found it last night and sent it off then. All eight pages of it."

"Something went wrong, then. I've been through Molly's email and it's not there."

"Email? What email? I faxed it."

"Faxed!" she echoed.

Travis sighed heavily. "Wake up, Stella. There's a fax number in Molly's email signature. Check her machine. I expect it's out of paper, or turned off. Just like Molly to let it go." He hung up.

Stella ran back into the office. "Molly! I didn't know you had a fax machine!"

"Sure." Molly appeared in the kitchen doorway, licking crumbs of fried chicken from her fingers. "I'm in business, of course I need a fax. Like I need email, 'cause not everybody texts or even phones. The fax is the kind where you use your regular phone line." She pointed. "There."

Molly's fax machine sat on a chair, one of the old set that belonged to the mahogany table, in a corner of the office/dining room. Stella bent over it. "There's paper here. Why isn't it turned on?"

"Oh, right. Hasn't been on for about a week. I guess I forgot about it, with all that's happened." Molly wiped her fingers on her jeans, reached past Stella and pressed the ON button.

The machine took a minute to warm up. Then it beeped and papers began spilling out into a plastic laundry basin on the floor below the chair. Molly gathered them up. "Order to purchase.... tree ornaments ... free trade shawls... oh-oh, an invoice ... 'nother invoice ... ad for efficiency software, like I need that... hey, what's this?"

Stella took the page from Molly's hand. It was covered with handwriting. The script was dim, as if the ink of the original had faded, but beautifully formed. Pages and pages followed each other into the basin.

"It's Lily's letter! It's huge!" Stella beamed at Molly. She felt flushed and light-headed with excitement. "And look, it's addressed to me!"

She would have sat down at the dining table then and there and started reading, but Molly put her hands over Stella's. "Hold on. For this we'll need proper chairs, food and drink."

They carried their chicken dinner to the book nook in the shop and moved cardboard boxes close to set out the food. Molly settled on the sofa with her feet up and a dinner box on her lap. Stella sat cross-legged in the armchair with the letter clutched in both hands.

"Now?" she demanded.

"Yes! Now." Molly waved regally. "Carry on."

Stella lifted the first page and began to read aloud. " 'My dear great-granddaughter Stella: When you read this you will be twelve years old...' "

Chapter 22

MY DEAR great-granddaughter Stella:

When you read this you will be twelve years old. Do me the courtesy, please, to read through to the end, no matter how strange it might seem to your young mind.

You will also have received two gold charms. Guard them well. Much more than an old woman's peace of mind depends on it.

First, a little about our family. The Craigs have been one of Glimmer's first families for more than a century. My father, Robert Craig, was both mine-owner and lawyer. I, the elder of his two daughters, was born in 1906. Aurora was born three years later: but, sadly, she lived at the cost of our mother's life. As I grew older, I assumed the role of mother to my young sister.

Aurora was not merely pretty. She was truly beautiful, with a bone-deep beauty that drew every eye. And with it she had grace and sparkle. Of course, we all expected her to make a brilliant match. Father envisioned a cabinet minister, at the very least, for a son-in-law. It was planned that she and I should, when Aurora neared eighteen, go to live with our maternal aunt in Toronto, where we would appear in good society and meet eligible young men.

It never came to be. The year Aurora turned sixteen, a young man named Heath Frost came to take up a position as mining engineer in father's company. He was intelligent, ambitious, and good-looking, but all too evidently sprung from the back streets. At once he was entranced by Aurora. She, for her part, found him amusing, and good company. That was no surprise. Compared to him, the local boys of good family seemed colourless. I quite enjoyed him, and found him attractive, but I knew he would never do for Aurora.

But very soon it became clear what Heath's intentions were. Aurora, light-hearted as ever, did nothing to discourage him. My father, worried that she might do something foolish and ruin her chances of marrying well, told Heath that he could not allow Aurora to marry before eighteen; and even then, he would frown on any suitor unable to support her as a lady of position.

Heath went away that autumn. Before he left, he promised Aurora that he would return in a year's time with a reputation and fortune fit to win a princess. She laughed and said she would like to see that, but promised nothing. My father, learning of it, said he hoped it was the last we would see of the interloper.

Aurora went on flirting, taking nothing and no one seriously, and a year passed. In late autumn of 1926, Heath returned. It was rumoured that he had travelled in the little-known lands between Europe and Asia. He was different, as everyone remarked. Certainly he was rich, and looked it: he showed that glossy assurance that comes with conscious wealth. But rather than being more brash and aggressive, as one might expect, he had become quiet and intent. In place of his sparkle was a deadly dark seriousness. And for those who knew how to see, there was a flicker of something extra, alien, in his face.

Aurora found the changed Heath fascinating, but repellent. Soon after his return, she told me that he was no longer amusing, and at times he frightened her.

After a week or so during which she avoided him, one afternoon he was able to catch her alone outdoors. It was my fault, and I shall blame myself forever. Aurora and I had gone to skate on the lake near the pavilion, and to see the party preparations. A freak wind (but I suspect it was no chance breeze) seized my hat and blew it toward the shore. I raced to catch it.

When I came skating back with my hat, I saw Heath and Aurora standing together. She looked dazed. A gold bracelet, one I had never seen before, shone on her left wrist. My heart lurched when I saw it, although I did not then know why.

Heath greeted me courteously enough. But at that moment I saw something gleam from his eyes: the same reflective flash that can be seen in a dog's eyes at night. It frightened me badly. I never clearly worked out what it meant, although I have my suspicions.

After that, Heath and Aurora were more and more together. She hardly spoke to anyone else, not even to me. She certainly never looked at any of the other young men.

There was consternation, but no great surprise, when Heath announced they would be married as soon as possible after her eighteenth birthday, and then they would go away and live in Europe, where his mysterious business concerns were located. Nothing Father said made any difference.

I stayed close to Aurora and, whenever I had opportunity, I studied the charm bracelet. It worried me more each day. It was only since she had put on the bracelet that she had changed. I sometimes had a Sight of the gold charms shining a viscous red, as if dipped in blood.

I thought of the change in Heath. When that rare greenish gleam flickered in his eyes, it seemed to me that more than one person looked out at me: that someone or something else was in there with him. I wondered where he had gone, and what he had paid — and to whom — to get that golden trinket.

I made up my mind that I must get my hands on it.

I should explain, great-granddaughter, that I have a gift. I don't refer to the Sight, which is common enough in our family among the women. I mean that I have a talent for reading objects. At a touch I can tell much about an object's age, nature, and history.

I did all I could to get within reach of the bracelet. But Aurora steadily refused to take it off, even for a moment. Nor would she let me touch it. And with each passing day, as I saw her turn exclusively to Heath, I was more and more sure that somehow the bracelet had put a shackle on her will and spirit.

So, one night, when everyone else in the house was asleep, I slipped into Aurora's room to steal the thing. My plan was first of all to learn its nature. If it proved harmful I would hide or destroy it. If I were mistaken and it proved safe, I would return it.

It was a night of bright moonlight, but the bedroom curtains were closed. When I came close to the bed, there was just enough moon glow to show where Aurora lay deeply asleep. Her left arm was out-flung, the wrist with the charm bracelet resting at the near edge of the bed. Something like a crumpled and heaped-up shawl lay on the white quilt next to her arm.

I knelt beside the bed and brought my hands close to the bracelet, to open the clasp. It should have been easy. But just before my fingers touched the clasp, the heap I had taken for a shawl stirred and uncurled. Eyes with a greenish gleam looked at me out of an animal head. It was something like a dog, although like no dog I had ever seen. The gleam in the eyes had been in Heath's eyes.

The dog rose and lunged at me. I fell back and cried out, and that woke Aurora. She demanded to know what I was doing there, what I was up to: her tone suspicious and hostile.

I dropped pretence and spoke of the creature I had seen (which was now nowhere visible), and my fears concerning Heath. That is, I tried to do so. She cut me off and refused to hear more, and I had no choice but to leave her room. I was not surprised to hear the key turn in the lock behind me. I did not sleep until dawn.

Now I knew for certain that Heath's gift to Aurora was cursed, and that it was working evil. I tried to convince her of this the next day, but she only laughed. Perhaps, she said, I coveted the pretty bracelet. Or possibly I was jealous. Perhaps I wanted Heath for myself. After that she would not let me near her. She spent the day in Heath's company, only returning that evening to dress for the party.

That night, December twenty-first, a grand Christmas party was held at the pavilion. There was a jazz band, decorated trees, coloured lights everywhere, bonfires on the shore; skating, dancing, carolling; hot drinks, little pastries, roasted nuts. A great joyful crowd of people gathered, most of them young as ourselves.

Among them were Aurora, Heath, and I. Aurora was the loveliest and brightest, Heath a knife-like shadow always at her elbow. I mingled quietly and danced, and watched for my chance. For two hours I watched and waited, and Heath never left her side. I began to lose hope.

It was because I was desperate that I did what I did next. I attacked Aurora from a distance, thinking hard at a cup of coffee on a nearby table until it tipped and spilled on her dress. Then I hurried forward to urge her into the ladies' cloak room, where I helped her sponge the stain from her skirt.

While I was moving about her, I managed to touch the bracelet. And then I was certain. This was dark, dark magic. No iron fetter could have been a stronger shackle than this. I wrenched at the chain and knew at once that the gold links, too, were under some control, because they should have given way easily. Instead, they held. Horror and fear — fear of Heath, for I felt him near, and coming nearer — gave me strength. I wrenched the charms free.

In that moment I knew I had done wrong. I had taken these spell-bound objects by force, and nothing good could come of that.

The ill effects began at once. When I opened my hand, I saw I had only two pendants. I thrust them into the pocket of my dress and looked for the other. It still hung on the bracelet on Aurora's wrist.

Removing two of the charms had at least cracked the fetter on Aurora's spirit. She became herself — almost. She was confused and hardly knew where she was. I might have been able to get the third charm then, but there was no time. Heath walked into the room.

Aurora grew white and clumsy with fear. She backed away, and he saw that he had lost his perfect control of her. As she fumbled to take off the bracelet, thinking perhaps to give it back to him, he threw back his head and howled.

That was when the pavilion cracked, crashed, and fell. Of course it had nothing to do with currents of water undermining the piles. It was Heath's rage, amplified by the something or someone extra inside him, that destroyed everything around him, breaching the foundation and bringing down the whole structure.

Of the many who died that night, Heath was the only one never found.

Aurora was drowned. When they pulled her out from under the ice, she was not wearing the sunburst charm. If it had been on her wrist I would have taken it, and then perhaps everything would have turned out differently. But the lake took it, and the ghosts kept it.

I was knocked unconscious by falling timbers, but was rescued: one of the "lucky" survivors, so they say. I recovered quickly, at least in body. And for a time I thought the story was over. I trusted that Aurora had gone on to a better world.

Then I began to see the dog-like creature shadowing me. And I dreamed of Aurora wearing the sun charm. She begged me to set her free. She tried to tell me how, but in the dreams Heath's spirit always stalked her and disrupted her attempts to speak. I learned only that the charms in my possession must be kept safe, and must be sent away from Glimmer (which I have done), lest Heath gain possession of them; that the power of the charms is in their unity; that if Heath regains control of the triple charm, Aurora's spirit will be chained to his forever, in whatever hell he inhabits.

There was more to learn, but I never learned it.

I am ashamed to say that I am no longer equal to the task of reversing this disaster, if ever I was. I could not save my sister's life and I could not free her spirit. That has been my great grief.

Ever since that terrible night in 1926 I have been haunted by those ghosts. You might wonder why I never went away. The reason I have stayed in Glimmer all this time is that I never quite lost hope of setting Aurora free. But after a few years the ghosts seemed to fade. I saw my sister only in vague, disturbing dreams in which nothing was communicated.

Now I must make several things clear to you.

What can I tell of the triple charm? That it is very, very old; that it is an object of great power, perhaps the talisman of some long-ago priestess. It is not evil in itself. (If it were, I would never have sent it to you!) In the wrong hands it could work great harm; in the right hands, great good. Heath used its power to enslave and hurt, but another could use that same power to liberate and heal.

Stella, take note of this. When it comes to power, and objects of power, you *must not simply take*. Such things must be given freely. If you take, you will be punished. That is how I lost my sister and why I have lived ever since with regret and grief.

And now my time grows short. I will soon be gone. Great-grand-daughter, I am passing my task to you. Not now, but when you come into your powers. You must finish what I began. But this time it *must be done right!*

If it is permitted, I will be with you in spirit.

God bless you.

With much love,

Lily Craig Macmillan

Chapter 23

STELLA LET the last page drop into her lap on top of the others. "Oh, wow...."

"No kidding!" Molly still held a chicken leg poised in the air. She had completely forgotten to eat while Stella was reading. "Do you realize how many different powers Lily was using? The Sight, telekinesis, divination of objects—"

"Yeah, great, but—" Stella felt as if she'd been dunked in cold water. "What the hell do I do now?"

"Well, we know more now about what we're up against. The letter does fill in a lot of gaps." Molly bit into the chicken leg.

"Not all of them, though." Stella collected the pages and shuffled them together. "Like, how can I get the sun charm if — what did she say? 'The lake took it and the ghosts kept it.' And if I do get it, what then? How am I supposed to free Aurora?"

"Mm-hm, and what's Heath going to be doing while all this is going on?" Molly licked her fingers. "Sitting on his hands? I don't think so."

"What really gets me—" Stella dropped the pages on the floor beside her chair. Now that the story had sunk in, she was overwhelmed. "Lily just shoved this onto me! When did I get a chance to say yes or no?"

"Hey, it's high praise! Obviously she believed you were the right person for the job."

"And that's another thing!" Stella clutched at her head. "'When you come into your powers,' she says. *What* powers?"

"Well, we know you do have some. And Lily believed—"

"Lily!" Stella shook her fists. "Molly, listen! Even Lily couldn't beat Heath! If she couldn't, what chance have I got?" She dropped her head into her hands. "I'm not sure I believe any of this!"

"Well, I do." Molly crossed the room, knelt by Stella's chair, and gave her a hug. "Look, you're just having a big fat case of nerves. I'll be there with you, and I've got tons of psychic energy I can lend you. I bet Mike does, too."

"Mike? I'm not so sure." Stella felt a pang of unease as she thought of him. She touched the two charms under her sweater. Their warm weight was reassuring.

"Speaking of boys who can dance, we'd better be getting ready." Molly began collecting dishes. "The party starts at 7:30, and if we're late we'll miss the mayor's speech!" She put on a look of mock horror. Stella giggled and felt her blue funk draining away.

"More important," she said, "I might miss Aurora. Let's move!"

STELLA DRESSED quickly in her new outfit, borrowing beige tights and a pair of high-heeled silver sandals from Molly.

Molly took longer. "Help me choose," she demanded, holding up three gauzy black dresses that all looked alike as far as Stella could see.

Stella wore no jewellery except the two pendants on their single gold chain. She had always kept her star charm covered, but now the two of them lay, for all to see, in the deep V of her neckline. Her hand went up to cover them. "I don't feel right, showing them off like this. I feel... well, nervous. Exposed."

"I know what you're thinking," Molly said soothingly. "But what difference does it make? I'm sure Heath doesn't need to see them to know where they are."

"Thanks, that makes me feel so much safer!"

They were ready, waiting by the door with their boots and coats on and their shoes in zippered bags, when the pickup truck pulled up in front of the house and the horn beeped. They stepped out into a wind that drove stinging snow pellets into their faces and tore at their hair.

They made a dash for the truck, Molly first. Stella piled in after her, slammed the door, pushed down her scarf and looked around. "Edge!"

"Yup, me." He put the truck in gear and headed back along the street.

"You shouldn't be out!" Molly studied his face. In the dashboard light he looked thin and ill. "Mike said you weren't up to par."

"Where *is* Mike?" Stella asked.

"I don't know."

"But he said," she faltered, thinking of that cold note in Mike's voice that afternoon. "He said he'd come to the party. Did he change his mind?"

"He didn't talk to me. He brought the truck home around five, then took the snowmobile. He didn't come in the house."

He's worried about Mike, Stella thought. She was worried too. Nobody said anything more.

Once they were on the Shore Road, following the curve of the lake, the driving became dangerous. Waves of snow turned the air white. Gusts of wind shook the truck and seemed bent on shoving it off the road into the ditch.

Edge drove slowly and carefully. He arrived at the pavilion ten minutes late, dropped them off, and stayed at the wheel. "I'm going to have a look round for Mike," he called through the closing door. The boom of wind in the pines nearly drowned out his voice.

Molly looked for a moment as if she was going to argue with him. Then she threw a kiss and waved him off. "I'm starting to know this guy," she shouted at Stella as they struggled through the blizzard to the pavilion. "There's no stopping him once he makes up his mind!" She sounded exasperated and fond at the same time, Stella thought. *Must be serious.*

The mayor was well into his speech when they arrived. The pavilion was full, the crowd buzzing quietly, the murmured chat all about the weather. They checked their coats, changed into their shoes, fixed their hair, and stepped out into the main hall just as the music started up.

"Looks like a great party." Stella looked around at the dancers bouncing and laughing to the tune of *Jingle Bell Rock* under the roof of misty golden light. The air smelled of cloves and hot cider, and the cedar boughs they'd tacked up that afternoon.

"Sad to say, you won't be able to relax and enjoy it. Hey, there's Joyce!" Molly waved as Joyce danced past with an older man who must be her husband.

"Too bad Mike's not here. Or Edge."

"That shouldn't stop us dancing, though." Molly was frankly casing the room. "Look at those two guys watching us from near the bar."

"Don't be silly, they're not watching us!"

"Oh, yes they are. The cute blond one's definitely giving you the eye." She lowered her voice. "And here they come!"

The two boys were sidling through the crowd toward them.

"But I—" Stella had been about to say she couldn't take the time to dance. Then she changed her mind. It occurred to her that dancing would be an easy and natural way to circulate around the hall. She'd never find Aurora just standing here.

It must make me a really boring person to dance with, though, she thought, some time later. Instead of smiling and talking with her partner, she kept scanning the crowd over his shoulder. Aurora never appeared.

The crowd thickened, the laughter grew louder, the music built in intensity. After about an hour, Stella was catching her breath next to one of the two big Christmas trees that glittered near the windows. Its resinous scent made her think of woods muffled in snow.

The window panes radiated cold. She shivered, rubbed her thinly covered arms, and listened to the night. Behind the happy noise of the crowd and the beat of music ran the bass song of wind in the pines. A gust slapped the building. The windows shook.

Her shoulder, brushing the window, felt suddenly wet and cold. She turned and stared at the window. *Ice? How did all that ice get there?*

She backed away from the window and bumped into Molly, who was dancing with the cute blond boy. "Molly! The weather's getting in!"

"Really?" Molly pulled to a stop. She gazed at the roof. "I don't see it. This is Tim, by the way."

"But listen!" Stella grabbed her arm. The whole building shook at a sudden violent gust.

"Oh, that's all right," Tim said. "They built it to give a little with the wind. That actually makes it stronger."

"Cool!" Molly leaned close to Stella and murmured: "Seen Aurora yet?"

"No. But—"

"All right. I'll keep my eyes peeled too." She steered Tim into the crowd.

Stella stood in a suddenly clear spot in the middle of the hall. The floor shook under her feet. She staggered. Cracks speared along the floorboards. Thick frost crept up the pillars and crusted the arches over the windows.

Nobody else seemed to notice. *People, look! Look!* The words stuck in her throat. A jagged hole appeared in the boards right in the centre of the hall. The gleam of dark water showed through. People danced past the hole as if it wasn't there.

The lights dimmed. The windows gaped empty. Snow whipped through the gaps. *It's turning into a ruin.* Stella recalled what Molly had said. She'd gone to the town council to protest the rebuilding of the pavilion, because she'd dreamed that "everybody died again."

Which horror was this? The old one? Or the one about to happen?

Got to warn them! She squeezed and elbowed through the crowd toward the band. There was a mike there. If she could only get hold of that, get their attention, get everybody out....

The band played on. People linked arms, forming a long line in front of the band, singing together, "We wish you a merry Christmas, we wish you..."

They pushed back when Stella tried to squeeze through the line. "You've got to let me through! Something terrible's happening!"

They laughed. She backed off and started around the outside of the hall.

And froze in mid-step. Across the room, a shadow slipped through the crowd at knee level. Its head moved as if tracking a scent.

She edged away among the dancers, came up with a thud against a solid body and spun around. Then nearly collapsed with relief. "Mike! Oh, I'm so glad!"

He smiled down at her. "Hello! Hey, you look as if you've had a shock."

"I saw the jackal! Over there!" Another couple bumped into them and circled away. Stella grabbed Mike's arm. "Better get out of here, we're a traffic hazard."

"Better idea. Let's dance!"

Next moment, they were gliding across the floor, smooth as quicksilver. After one astonished moment, Stella relaxed into Mike's arms. Everything seemed all right again. Even the jackal no longer seemed all that scary. Had she actually seen it?

"You weren't just boasting, were you? You really can dance!"

He laughed softly. "I'm famous for it."

"But where've you been? Edge has been worried about you! And something…. something's going wrong." She closed her eyes briefly, trying to focus. "The pavilion… it's breaking down. It's starting to look like the old ruin…"

"Is it? Look again."

She opened her eyes and looked past his arm. The floor was uncracked, the windows intact, no sign of frost or ice anywhere.

"But I was so sure something awful was about to happen!"

"Well, it isn't. Relax, Stella-Star. Enjoy the night!"

She laughed, flying on a sudden wave of euphoria. "Is this what you'd call mojo?"

"Could be." His voice smiled, his breath was warm against her ear.

How he'd changed! Gone was the worried, tired, not-very-artic-ulate boy with the rare smile. This Mike is amazing, she thought dreamily. She leaned her head on his shoulder and closed her eyes again. She was dancing on stars, each note of the music a spark of gold.

"If only we could dance like this forever," she murmured.

"Why can't we?"

"Oh, I wish…"

Something small, hard, and oddly heavy poked her in the breastbone. It nudged a memory into the open. *Oh, right: the pendants. Aurora.* Stella sighed and pushed lightly away from Mike. His arm tightened around her waist. "Got things to do," she said softly.

"Let 'em go," he murmured against her hair.

"Can't…"

"Then let me help."

"You've already helped a lot." She raised her head. "Mike, Aurora said…"

"Let me look out for Aurora. Share this chore. Let me carry the charms."

The charms. Strange how very heavy they were, suddenly. No reason not to share the burden, was there? "I… I suppose…."

Only, only… Lily had saddled the task on her, and only her.

His hand slid up her back toward the nape of her neck. "Yes. Say yes."

There was a new, greedy note in his voice. Stella felt as if she'd got a faceful of wet snow. Her head cleared. She stumbled, no more stars under her feet.

She pulled him to a stop. "Mike? What's wrong?" And looking into his eyes, she saw they were no longer that soft, warm brown. Deep down, a green gleam flickered and was gone. Her heart seemed to stick in her throat.

"Oh, Mike! Not you!"

His hands tightened. She wrenched away and dodged in among the crowd. They opened and closed again around her, laughing and singing. A glance back: he was slipping through after her.

"Lily! Over here!"

Stella looked around, startled. A golden-haired girl in a short silk dress reached out and clasped her hand. Stella only had time to think, *She's real!* And then the lights and dancers blurred.

In the last split second Molly's voice called her name, and a hand closed on her wrist.

When she could see straight once more, everything had changed. The clothes, the decorations, the music, even the lights were different. Everything seemed softer, more mellow.

It was December 21, 1926. That other, doomed party was in full swing. The six-man jazz band beside the bar was playing *Bye Bye Blackbird*, and the boys and girls shimmying across the dance floor had been dead for nearly ninety years.

Chapter 24

STELLA HAD half a second to take it in when a couple danced straight at her — and then straight through her. A cold breeze swept through her flesh and bones. She shuddered. *Ghosts.*

"No, they're not ghosts, not really."

She looked up to see the golden-haired girl smiling at her. "In this place, you're the ghost. Because you don't belong." Aurora's eyes flicked over Stella's shoulder. "Nor do they." She lifted a hand to point, and the bracelet, with its one dangling charm, gleamed on her left wrist.

Stella turned to look. She flinched. Mike was standing behind her, just beyond arm's reach. He had Molly pinned against him with one arm. With the other hand he was tracing a suggestive line across her throat.

"I'm sorry," Molly whispered. "He came through with me. I couldn't shake him off."

"Let her go!" Stella snapped. "She can't help you."

"Of course she can." The green gleam was very bright in his eyes. "She's my purchase price. Your sister's life is worth a couple of gold trinkets, don't you think?"

Molly's face looked blank, whether from courage or terror wasn't clear. Stella's heart thumped. "You don't need her! Let her go! Just take the things, why don't you?" She clenched her fists. "Or aren't you strong enough?"

Mike's eyes narrowed. A dog-like shape padded forward from behind him. Two couples danced across the space, straight through the jackal. It didn't so much as flick an ear. Its too-intelligent eyes never left Stella's face.

She backed away, arms spread wide. "Come on, try and take them! Just try!" For each step back she took, the jackal took one step forward. Fangs showed white points under the wrinkling lip.

Foolhardy. Crazy! But each step took her closer to Aurora. Close enough, and Aurora could slip her the sun charm. And then, with the combined power of the triple charm....

"Take them? No, I know better than that." Mike smirked, and the jackal sat down, its tongue lolling. "I learned my lesson from Lily. Take the charms by force, and you get punished. No, what you'll do..."

His right hand tightened on Molly's throat and she choked. Stella started forward, but instantly the jackal was up and coming at her, head down, chest rumbling, fangs bared.

"It can't hurt me," she quavered, wishing she sounded more confident. Another couple danced through her space. A black sleeve breezed through her arm, a sparkling eye passed right though her own, making her flinch and shut her eyes tight. "That animal — it's no more real than they are!"

Mike laughed harshly. Why, she wondered, didn't I notice right at the start that his voice is nothing like Mike's natural voice?

"That *animal* is more real than anything here," he said. "More real than you or me. But never mind that. The charms: I want them. You'll give them to me."

"They wouldn't be freely given."

"Of course they would. It would be your free choice. Molly or the charms." He let go of Molly's throat and held out his hand, palm up.

She stared at it, mentally searching round and round for another way out. *Like a rat in a trap.*

"And it wouldn't be just Molly. I could kill this thing too." He touched his own smiling face. "Your dear Mike. And not just them. All those people in the pavilion tonight — your pavilion in your time, not this one — dancing away without a care in the world. I could kill them all."

"No!" Molly whispered.

Stella felt as if he'd punched her in the stomach. Joyce. Bonnie. Tim. All the boys and girls she didn't know. Molly's neighbours, decent people. "You wouldn't. You couldn't!"

"I could and I would. Picture it! It would be just like it was in Lily's day. Right, Lily?" He thrust a look like a dagger past Stella's shoulder. *Lily?* She had no time to look back. "Like this!" Mike said, and he threw back his head and howled, and the jackal howled with him.

The music broke off with a wail of trumpets. The roof beams cracked. The floor gave way. Glass shattered, water spurted up from below. The dancing crowd became a screaming tangle of human bodies, all clinging to each other, all struggling to save or be saved.

Stella covered her ears and shut her eyes. "Stop! Please stop!"

The terrible screaming and crashing faded. Stella dared to open her eyes. They stood in the same hall, but it was later. How much time had passed? Weeks or years? There was no way of knowing.

The roof was gone. The floor was a puzzle of cracked boards and jagged holes. The moon glistened on ice-draped arches and frost-crusted beams.

Molly was crying into her hands. Mike was smiling.

"You see? I could do it just like that." He flicked a hand. "All that will happen unless you give me what you hold, Stella-Star. And you alone will be left to bear the blame."

Stella shook her head. This was not the way it was supposed to turn out! Aurora was supposed to hand over the sun charm, and then with the power of the triple charm they were going to free her and send Heath back to the hell he came from.

Not that, a soft voice breathed in her ear. *Heath is a prisoner too.*

A cool hand touched hers and something small and warm slid into her palm. *Aurora?* Stella didn't dare look around. She moved her eyes from Mike to the jackal and back again.

Save him too.

Stella looked into her hand. The sun-shaped charm glittered up at her. Mike snarled and took a clumsy step forward, pulling Molly with him. The jackal crouched as if to spring.

"Stay where you are!" Stella snapped. "I could turn you into a fruit fly with this."

"Try." Mike showed his teeth. "You'd lose everything."

In a few swift movements she unclasped the chain from around her neck, slid the sun pendant onto it with the others, and wrapped the chain around her right hand, with the triple charm safe in her fist. *Now what?*

Another voice, not so soft, whispered behind her. *Strike a bargain, great-granddaughter.*

Lily? She just barely stopped herself from spinning around.

I did say I would be with you in spirit. Be ready for anything.

"Communing with spirits?" Mike gave Molly a shake that made her head flop back and forth. "Hurry up! I'm losing patience."

"All right!" Stella held up both fists. "You win. I'll give you the triple charm."

"No!" Molly cried out.

Mike laughed in triumph and again held out his hand. "Finally!"

Stella folded her arms. "Not yet. Not until you let everybody go."

"What?" Mike squinted at her. "What do you mean, everybody?"

"What I said. Start with Molly."

"And lose my purchase price?" He snorted. "Likely!"

Give your word, said the cool whisper behind Stella's shoulder.

"My word?" she echoed, startled.

Mike narrowed his eyes. "You will swear?" His voice didn't sound remotely like Mike's any more. "Good. Do it. Swear by Molly's life. And believe me, I will hold you to it."

Stella took a deep breath and avoided looking at Molly, who was fiercely mouthing something at her. "All right. I swear by Molly's life that I will give you the triple charm — *after* you have set *all* your prisoners free."

Mike stared as if he was trying to drill holes in her skull with his eyes. The jackal growled steadily. Can it read my mind? she wondered.

"Go on, then!" Mike gave Molly a push. She stumbled, skidded on the frost-coated floorboards, caught her balance, and scurried over to grab Stella's arm.

Stella nodded. "Now set Mike free."

"This thing!" Mike slapped his own face and laughed. "Well, all right, it's no use to me now." The moment the last word was out of his mouth, his face went blank. He dropped to his knees, then fell onto his face on the splintery floor, limp as an empty suit of clothes.

"Mike!" He didn't stir. Was he still alive? Stella was itching to run to him. She would have, if not for the man who stood facing her now. He was tall, like Mike, but there the resemblance ended.

Heath inclined his dark head with deadly courtesy. He beckoned. "Now," he said, in a voice like a lion's purr.

Stella clenched her shaking hands. "*All* your prisoners, I said. Heath too."

"What?" Molly squeaked.

Heath's eyebrows flicked up. The jackal's jaws parted in a grin. "Me!" Heath shook his head, laughing. "I'm no prisoner. I made a choice, and in return I gained wealth, power, and the woman I loved — for a little while. Until Lily stole her from me." His voice darkened.

The jackal took a step forward and looked straight into Stella's face. It opened its mouth and spoke with Heath's voice. "And now I will have her again. Forever."

Silence held for three of Stella's flurried heartbeats. A moonlit snowflake drifted down. Into the stillness Heath said casually: "Keep your word, or see your sister die."

Molly's fingers dug into her wrist. *What now?* Stella asked the air.

Keep your word, of course.

Stella held out her fist and slowly opened her fingers. The triple charm was warm and heavy, and seemed to stick to her palm. The jackal took another step forward, opening its jaws. Another step, and it was growing larger. Another step ....

But not in this place. A hand gripped Stella's other wrist. *Molly, hold tight!*

The ruined pavilion blurred.

Chapter 25

THE THREE of them stood alone on a flat, white plain under a black sky. Snow whipped at their faces. It must be a frozen lake, Stella thought. The shore made a dark border all around, low in the far distance.

The howling wind hurled sheets of snow past their heads. Stella automatically clasped her arms for warmth, then dropped her hands when she realized she wasn't cold. And now she thought about it, the wind wasn't even stirring her hair.

"Lily!" Molly did a happiness dance in the snow. "I knew it had to be you!"

Lily looked the way she had in the photo taken with Aurora. A tall girl, the same height as Stella, clear eyes that looked directly at you, short brown hair smoothed back and untroubled by the wind. She was looking at Molly now the way you'd look at a badly behaved four-year-old.

Molly spread out her arms and twirled to make her black draperies fly. The snow billowed around her without settling on her. "That's so cool! Wish I could get that to happen at home."

"We are not here to amuse ourselves."

Stella felt intimidated by Lily but wasn't going to let it show. "So, why *are* we here?"

"And where is *here*?" Molly put in.

Lily didn't seem inclined to answer. There was no sign of any human dwelling in all that flat, barren landscape. No lights showed anywhere. Stella tilted back her head and scanned the sky. No star, no moon. She shivered, but not from cold.

"Shouldn't we be going somewhere?" Molly looked around uneasily.

The only other thing to be seen besides themselves was a black dot, small with distance, that separated from the dark shore and began moving toward them across the frozen lake. Molly pointed. "What's that?"

"The jackal, of course," Lily said. "And no, we're not going anywhere. One spot is as good as another in this place."

"Lily." Stella touched her arm. She half expected her hand to pass through a column of cold air and out the other side. But Lily's arm felt as real as her own. "Was that you..."

Lily looked back at her with a hint of twinkle in the stern eyes. "In your dreams? Calling you? Yes, and it was no easy task getting your attention! You're a deep sleeper."

"And the books?" Molly ventured.

"That too. I did think you were both a little slow."

Stella looked across the lake. The black dot was nearer now, moving steadily. "You haven't said where we are. And why did we leave the pavilion to come here?"

"Yeah," Molly said. "I thought it was to get away from that!" She pointed at the black dot, which now clearly looked like what it was.

"Very well." Lily kept her eyes fixed on the jackal. "You don't need to know this, but I'll tell you. The pavilion is built on a site of unstable power. The jackal could easily use that instability, it could tilt it to its own advantage. This...." She nodded her head around at the empty snowscape. "This is a neutral place. It's no place at all, really. Time doesn't pass, night and winter never end. It's a level plane, where power is concerned."

Molly moved closer to Stella. "So, we can beat him here? We're not really going to give him the charm, are we?"

"We must. The oath Stella swore can't be broken without disaster. I don't suppose you want to die before your time," she added drily.

"Well, of course not, but—" Molly danced out in front of her and shook her clenched hands. "But what about Aurora? Aren't there spells you know? You're a powerful witch—"

"Nonsense!" Lily wasn't listening, Stella thought. She was too intent on the approaching hunter. It was growing bigger as it came nearer: bigger than she remembered it being.

"But she's your sister!" Molly yelled. "You can't just let him have her!"

Lily grabbed Molly by the wrist. "It's almost here. Be ready!"

Stella posted herself at Lily's other side. "There's a reason why we're three, isn't there? I mean, three's the charm, power of three... This looks like a blasted heath, all right." She heard herself babbling and shut up.

Molly laughed too brightly. "Double, double toil and—"

"Steady!" Lily snapped. "Follow my lead. Remember our blood bond. And have courage!"

The jackal was a few strides away, swift, fanged jaws opening.

"Stella," Lily said calmly. "I think now would be a good time, don't you?"

"But what should I—" And then there was no time left at all. Stella wound up and hurled the triple charm high in the air. It was the only thing she could think of, a useless delaying tactic. The golden cluster shone like a star against the roof of dark cloud, then dropped. The jackal leaped and snapped it up in its jaws.

"Circle!" Lily cried. And wheeling smoothly like birds in a flock, the three began pacing, one after the other, hands linked. And they were singing, although Stella hadn't heard anyone call for song. At least, Lily was singing and Molly was humming, Stella couldn't make out what.

The jackal, with the gold chain looped across its grinning jaws, dropped into the circle they were marking out in the snow. But how? Stella wondered. Surely it was far too big to fit. Was it getting smaller?

Around and around they stepped in a smooth, sliding dance. The jackal snarled and kept turning to keep each face in view. The trough they marked in the snow seemed to hold it like a fortress wall.

Why doesn't it just bite? Stella wondered. It could take my leg off with those jaws. Why doesn't it jump out?

Round and round they stepped in their measured rhythm, and Stella realized she was singing too, they were singing together. One moment it was *Guide Me O Thou Great Jehovah*, and three steps on she thought it was *All Around the Mulberry Bush*, and soon after that she heard herself chanting *We Will, We Will Rock You*.

So that's what Lily's made of us, Stella thought, in a quiet moment that visited her between breaths. *The three of us together, our powers combined, we are a triple charm. A human talisman. Just like...* She thought of Molly's little herbal bundles wrapped in scarlet floss. *Red, the colour of life. A triple charm bound by blood. How strong would that be?*

Inside the circle, the trapped creature began to howl. The sound ripped through Stella's head. Molly staggered, but Stella caught her and so did Lily, and they danced on, hand in hand, step after step, round and round.

And now they were singing in no language Stella knew, in a tune she'd never heard before. But it crossed her mind that the morning stars might have sung that song together, sometime very long ago.

The creature howled, and crouched, and now Stella was sure. It was smaller. It was changing. Not so much like a jackal now: more like some snaky, ferrety animal. And then thinner still, and longer, and....

It was a snake. A strong-bodied golden snake that raised its head and fixed its shining green eyes on them as they danced and sang around it. And then, with a lightning motion, it drilled its head straight down at the snow. Its body followed its head into the hole, coil after coil, until finally its pointed tail slithered down into the dark.

The singing trailed off. The dancers slowed and stopped. They stood around a small hole in the snow. Snow drifted across and the hole became a dent, and then there was no mark at all.

Molly was the first to speak. "Is it gone? Did we beat it?"

Lily let out a long breath. "It's gone. Not beaten. That's not something we can beat, not by ourselves. But we've won this particular battle."

She bent down and scooped up something from the snow. A gold chain dangled from her fingers, hung with three gold pendants. She held it out to Stella. "You take charge of this. We still have some unfinished business to complete."

Stella wound the chain around her hand. She took a last look around this place of perpetual night and winter. "Right. Let's get back." She looked at Lily, eyebrows raised. "You, um, do know how to get us back?"

SHE CAUGHT her breath. "Okay, I guess you do."

Molly and Stella stood clutching hands near the bar in the new pavilion. No mistake, it was their own place and time. The hall rang with music and laughter.

Stella sagged with relief. "I think, in the back of my mind, I was afraid..."

"I know." Molly gave her a quick hug. "Me too. But everything's okay!"

The improvised choir had added half a dozen new singers and was working on *Winter Wonderland*.

Stella blinked and rubbed her eyes. For one blurred moment she saw the snowy lake, the ice-crusted ruin, and the ghostly dancers from 1926, all drifting like plumes of fog through and through each other, and through the reality and colour around her. A jazz rendition of *Bye Bye Blackbird* tangled discordantly with the music of the other song for a moment before fading.

Then the confusion cleared, and there was Mike shouldering through the crowd toward them. "You're all right?" he demanded, looking Stella over from head to toe.

As if it wasn't obvious. "Never better!"

"Whoah!" He rubbed his temples. "When you just vanished like that, I was afraid..." He dropped his hands. "And the jackal?"

"Gone."

"And we've won!" Molly danced a little.

Stella didn't feel it necessary to add "this time, anyway." She opened her hand to show the triple charm. Mike slipped his arms around her and gave her a fierce hug. Her breath went out in a huge whoosh.

"You had me damn worried," he muttered in her ear.

"No more worried than me! How long were we away?"

"Only a few minutes, I think. But look who's turned up!" He pointed.

Edge was stepping carefully through the crowd. His face lit up when he saw Molly, who whooped and rushed to grab and hug him.

"Where's Lily?" Stella looked around. "She should be here. She said there was still unfinished business to be done."

"Um…" Mike was staring out the window. "Would that be her?"

Stella looked, and then realized Mike had never before seen any of the three who were gathered out on the deck. If you gave them more than a passing glance, you'd notice that you could see the guard rail through their heads. No wonder he looked nervous. It wasn't every day you saw a ghost, let alone three at once.

Aurora and Heath sat side by side in the snow, like picnickers on grass. "Funny," Stella murmured. "What are they doing together, those two? And why is he still here?"

"Look at him," Molly said.

Lily was kneeling beside them, her lips moving, soundless behind the glass. Heath looked up at her. His face… "Hard to believe he's the same person," Molly said.

"He isn't," Stella said. "He's himself as he used to be. As he was meant to be."

"Not," Edge said quietly, "whatever the jackal made of him."

They watched Heath turn his head to look at Aurora. An expression of great love and terrible sadness settled on his face. He spoke and she answered. She smiled. They took each other's hands.

"We freed him, too." Stella cleared her throat, which was suddenly clogged. "We freed them all."

Lily looked over her shoulder through the glass at Stella and beckoned.

"All right, they want me out there." She was moving toward the nearest exit as she spoke.

"You'll freeze!" Mike followed her. "Wait, I'll get your coat."

"No, no time! And don't come with me." She looked Mike in the eye, then Edge, then Molly, who frowned. "Not any of you."

Out on the deck the storm still howled and raged. Stella shuddered with cold and fought to catch her breath. "W-will this t-take long? B-because I—"

"Not long," Lily said briskly, not a hair stirring. "You must finish what I began. Send us where we belong. That charm bound us all, you see, though in different ways."

Stella opened her stiff fingers with difficulty. The triple charm seemed to have cooled. It wasn't keeping her anywhere near warm. "O-okay, b-b-but h-how?"

"*I* don't know." Lily gave her an impatient look.

"Isn't th-there s-some s-spell you sh-sh-should t-t-teach—"

"Spell? Don't be silly. Use your common sense. And keep it simple!"

Common sense. All right. "G-good bye, all of you. L-lily..." There was so much more she wanted to say, so many questions she wanted to ask, but Lily waved at her to get on with it.

"Now, girl!"

Now. Stella clasped the triple charm in her right hand. Its warmth suddenly bloomed and surrounded her. She looked from face to face, not wanting to forget any one of them. Aurora's gently smiling loveliness, Heath's expression of incredulous hope. Lily's clear-cut features, at once fond and severe.

"It's time," Stella said. "Go home."

Snow whirled through empty air where three people had been.

In the pavilion behind her, the improvised choir was singing *Silent Night.*

Chapter 26

TWO DAYS before the new year, Molly and Stella sat in a window booth in Bonnie's Good Eats waiting for the Toronto bus to pull in to the curb on Queen Street.

"It's been a great visit!" Molly nursed a mug of tea in her hands. "I mean, it's been great since the twenty-first. I wish you could stay longer. There's still so much we need to talk about."

"Like?" Stella dug into a plate of eggs, bacon, potato pancakes and fried onions. She guessed it would be her last chance of real food for the next twenty-four hours.

"Like, why Lily refused to admit she was Wiccan, deep down. It was so obvious she was a powerful white witch."

"That doesn't make her Wiccan. What I'm wondering..." Stella pointed her fork at Molly. "...is what she meant about the pavilion standing on a site of unstable power."

"And what was that frozen place where she took us to meet the jackal?"

There was more Stella wondered about. What had actually happened in that place of endless night? What had they done, the three of them? How had they defeated something so strong and so evil? And what was that last song they'd sung?

She wasn't sure she really wanted any of the answers. Not yet. So she didn't ask Molly. And Molly had been strangely silent on those questions herself.

"Still got the triple charm, I see." Molly nodded at Stella's collar, where a few links of the gold chain were visible.

"Think I'd lose it?"

"I was wondering…" Molly took a sip of tea, then set down her cup. "…what you're planning to do with it."

"Nothing. Keep it safe." Stella pushed away her plate. "Why? You want it back?"

"No way! It's strong mojo, as Mike would say. Too strong for me. Dangerous."

"Exactly why I don't plan to let anyone else have it." Power to liberate and heal, Lily had said. In the right hands. *Are mine the right hands?*

"Well, be careful. And don't throw away those extra-strength herbal bundles I stuck in your bags."

"More herbs? Molly, for the love of—"

"Oops, here comes the bus!" Molly found her wallet, slapped money on the table, and jumped up from the booth. Then leaned to the window. "And speaking of mojo, there's Mike!"

They lugged Stella's bags to the curb. Molly hugged Stella, growling "Hate goodbyes!" in her ear. Then waggled her eyebrows at Mike and ran off up the street, leaving Stella pink-cheeked and at a loss for words.

The two of them stood side by side, dumbly watching the other travellers board. When they spoke, their words collided. "Well, it's been nice—" "Wish there'd been more time—" They broke off together and laughed.

Mike cleared his throat. "Too bad British Columbia's such a long way away."

"Oh, I'll be back. Molly seems set on staying here."

"That's good. I'm applying for a scholarship to the University of Waterloo. Engineering."

"Cool! Good school." Her heart felt like lead. *I'll never see him again.*

"But you'll probably fall over me at family gatherings," he said casually, watching the driver stow Stella's bags in the luggage hold. "Seeing that I'm likely to be your brother-in-law."

"What!" She spun and stared at him. "D'you have inside information I don't have?"

"Uh-uh." He shook his head, smiling.

"All aboard!" the driver called.

"Don't tell me you have the Sight! I don't think I could stand that."

He laughed. "You don't have to be psychic to see—"

The bus engine started with a roar. "Better go!" Mike shouted.

Stella leaped for the door, climbed the steps, sidled along the aisle, and dropped into the last empty seat. Mike was standing right below her window. She pressed her face to the glass.

Mike, she moved her lips without sound. *I'll miss you.*

He smiled up at her. His eyes were as warm as summer.

She mimed thumb-texting. He nodded vigorously. The bus started up.

Just before it pulled away, he reached up and set his hand on the window. She laid her hand on his, fingers matching, the cold glass between them.

And for a moment there was no glass. His hand pressed on hers, warm skin on warm skin.

Then he was gone. But it seemed to her she still felt his palm against hers, long after a hundred icy miles lay between them.

About the author

PATRICIA BOW lives in Kitchener, Ontario. She has written more than twenty books for readers of all ages who love mystery, suspense and fantasy. To find out more about Patricia and her work, visit her web page at www.execulink.com/~thebows/patricia.htm.